Hanoverian Succession

Elizabeth = Frederick, Elector Palatine

All issue barred
but daughter Sophia = Ernest, Elector
of Hanover

Henriette = Philip, Duc d'Orleans
(Brother of Louis XIV)

George I
(1714–1727)

Anne Marie = Victor Amadeus,
Duke of Savoy

Issue barred

Sovereigns of Britain are in **boldface,** with their reigns in parentheses

(*Issue barred* means issue disqualified from succeeding to the Crown—
decreed by Parliament for religious reasons)

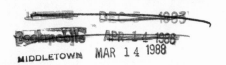

Also by Louis Auchincloss

FICTION

The Indifferent Children
The Injustice Collectors
Sybil
A Law for the Lion
The Romantic Egoists
The Great World and Timothy Colt
Venus in Sparta
Pursuit of the Prodigal
The House of Five Talents
Portrait in Brownstone
Powers of Attorney
The Rector of Justin
The Embezzler
Tales of Manhattan
A World of Profit
Second Chance
I Come as a Thief
The Partners
The Winthrop Covenant
The Dark Lady
The Country Cousin
The House of the Prophet
The Cat and the King
Watchfires
Narcissa and Other Fables

NONFICTION

Reflections of a Jacobite
Pioneers and Caretakers
Motiveless Malignity
Edith Wharton
Richelieu
A Writer's Capital
Reading Henry James
Life, Law and Letters
Persons of Consequence: Queen Victoria
and Her Circle

EXIT
LADY
MASHAM

Louis Auchincloss

HOUGHTON MIFFLIN COMPANY BOSTON
1983

Library of Congress Cataloging in Publication Data

Auchincloss, Louis.
    Exit Lady Masham.

    1. Masham, Abigail, Lady, 1684 or 5–1734—Fiction.
2. Anne, Queen of Great Britain, 1665–1714—Fiction.
I. Title.
PS3501.U25E9   1983   813′.54   83–319
ISBN   0–395–34388–7

Printed in the United States of America

D   10   9   8   7   6   5   4   3   2   1

A signed first edition of
this book has been privately
printed by The Franklin Library.

TO BARBARA W. TUCHMAN,
who has made history more fascinating
than any fiction

PART ONE

1

Oates Manor
Buckinghamshire
November, 1733

*I*t was Lord Hervey who persuaded me to embark on these memoirs. So strong an impression did he make on me that here I am, only a week after his suggestion, taking up my pen.

"Don't put it off, Lady Masham, I beg of you," he urged me. "You owe it to history. Those of us who were privileged to view the making of great events have the duty to record them. Some of the mightiest monarchs survive to posterity only in the pages of humble scribes. George II and Queen Caroline will have Hervey. Queen Anne will have Your Ladyship."

"You forget you're talking to an old woman. I may not have the time."

"I don't consider fifty-three old."

"So you've looked me up!"

"That is a penalty of fame."

"Fame! Admit, my friend, that your good Queen Caroline would not have asked me to come to court today had you not piqued her curiosity by telling her my story. Isn't that true? She had never heard of me, had she?"

"My dear lady, what does that prove? The Queen was raised in a petty German court and knows nothing but Teutonic history. Still, we must give her credit. She wants to learn, and she never forgets. Most German princesses are absolutely hopeless. She was recalling the other day what her mother had replied to our minister to Anspach when he suggested that her daughter should learn the tongue of the nation that her betrothed husband would one day rule. 'Ach, there's no sense to that! After the Hanover family have been on the throne another year or so, the English will all speak German.' It is true that it was I who first brought your name to Her Majesty's attention, but she listened with the greatest interest to your story. And, of course, every English schoolchild has heard of you."

"The way they've heard of the Battle of Hastings. As something ancient and remote from their daily lives. Oh, yes, I understood those glances in court today, Lord Hervey! 'Who is that? Lady Masham? You don't mean the friend of Queen Anne? Is *she* still alive?' "

"Well, I'd be the last man in the world to deny the shortness of a courtier's memory. But some people recall more than you suppose. And it wasn't *that* long ago, anyway. When did Queen Anne die? In 1714? Why, that's not a score of years back."

"It seems more to one who has hardly been away from Oates Manor in all that time. I feel like Hermione in *The Winter's Tale*. I am stepping down from my pedestal into a new world. And not one, I fear, that I like very much."

"All the more reason to keep the past alive."

"Well, the country mouse will think about it, Lord Hervey, when she's back in her quiet nest."

As this manuscript will not be published in my lifetime — and certainly never, if my husband survives me — I should explain who Lord Hervey is. He is the court chamberlain whom Queen Caroline dotes on, quite as if he were her own son. Much more so, actually, for both she and King George are reputed to detest the Prince of Wales. It is generally believed that Sir Robert Walpole depends on Lord Hervey to keep the Queen in line politically when she is acting as regent during the frequent visits of her spouse to his beloved Hanover. But more important, at least to me, the chamberlain is supposed to be the most beautiful and charming man at court. They say he bewitches both sexes, that husbands forgive him for lying with their wives and even their mistresses. It is notorious that he is the father of Miss Vane's last child, whom the Prince of Wales is raising as his own bastard!

Out of the blue I received a letter from Lord Hervey three weeks ago, instructing me that Her Majesty desired to make my acquaintance and appointing the day on which I was summoned to St. James's Palace. I had become so accustomed to my quiet life in the country, with my back firmly turned on courts and palaces, that it required a considerable resolution to overcome my inertia and obey.

Everything at St. James's seemed much the same as in the old days, except for the presence of many more guards, a symptom, not of George II's fear of assassination, but of his passion for the military. Lord Hervey, who met my chair by the gate, was even more charming than I had anticipated. He escorted me to where Queen Caroline, with the Princesses Caroline and Emily, was receiving at a late afternoon drawing room. After I had made my curtsy I was invited to sit with the royal group. The Queen, a robust, straight-backed woman, who may have been pretty when she was young, addressed me in the gruff, direct German manner.

"I am most interested in the court of Queen Anne, Lady Masham. It seems to have been a women's paradise. All the favorites were ladies!" Here she laughed, rather crudely, and glanced at her daughters, as if to suggest that such an anomaly could have existed only in England. "Is it true that the Queen and the Duchess of Marlborough addressed each other as 'Mrs. Jones' and 'Mrs. Smith'?"

"Not quite, ma'am. Her late Majesty adopted the sobriquet of 'Mrs. Morley,' while the Duchess chose the surname 'Freeman.' "

"And did they call each other 'Mrs. Morley' and 'Mrs. Freeman' in public?"

"Oh, no, ma'am, never. That was only for their private use. They desired to ease the *gêne* that may exist between sovereign and subject."

"Really! I cannot imagine a German royalty permitting such a liberty. And yet I do not believe that any *gêne* exists between me and those whom I like and trust. Is it not so, Lord Hervey?" She turned to her chamberlain with what seemed as close to a wink as a Teutonic princess could emulate. "He tells me of his *amours*, the naughty boy! The late Queen and her beloved Duchess must have been like two old village gossips. And it was you, Lady Masham, who broke up that famous friendship? How did you do it?"

My disgust with the House of Hanover was so strong at this point that I was at a loss for words. Had the Pretender at that junction appeared in the doorway, I think I should have knelt to him, even at the risk of my head! But at last I managed to find my tongue and to murmur something about the rupture between myself and the Duchess having been of the latter's seeking.

"But what had she against you?" the Queen persisted. "That you had stolen Queen Anne's heart?"

Another coarse laugh, and another *oeillade* to the Princesses, showed me clearly enough how the Queen construed my relationship to Anne of England. I tried to keep my composure by reminding myself that it was not the first time that I had been subjected to such insinuations.

"I can only repeat, ma'am, that you must go to my cousin for your answer."

"Your cousin? The great Duchess is your cousin? I thought you had been only a bedchamber woman to the late Queen. I shall never understand your English families."

"They *are* confusing, ma'am. They keep going up and down. We cannot boast the stability of the continent."

Fortunately, the royal circle now opened to welcome the King's mistress, Lady Deloraine, and the old "favorite" of Queen Anne's days was quickly forgotten. It was on my way out of the palace, escorted by the still solicitous Lord Hervey, that the colloquy took place that I have recorded. At the end of it, when I was in my chair and about to be borne away, I did a strange thing. It is the kind of thing that any lonely, forgotten old woman may do when confronted with a man who is young and beautiful and kind to her. I seized his hand and imprinted my lips on it.

✤

As I look about the world today, I begin to see what Lord Hervey meant. The group of persons who exercised political power in the last four years of Queen Anne's reign have disappeared so completely from the London scene that it is almost as if they had never existed. And look at the ones who have *not* disappeared. Look at the people who in 1711 were supposed to have been swept out of power by the "Tory clique," headed by Robert Harley and Henry St. John, and assisted by the wily Abigail Hill, that sly hussy who managed to turn herself into "Lady Masham." Those who were ostensibly defeated seem now to have embedded themselves in the

golden fabric of English glory, while the Tory clique has
been relegated to obscurity or disgrace. Who today has heard
of Abigail? What is St. John but a pardoned traitor? Or
Harley but a drunken and now dead politician? Yet old
Sarah, the widowed Duchess of Marlborough, is holding court
at Blenheim Palace as splendidly as any queen. She has become the very symbol of our late victories abroad, and her
deceased warrior-husband is our national hero and legend.
The days of the Marlborough ascendancy in the reign of
Queen Anne are deemed by many the finest pages in our
history.

I suppose I should have expected all this. My illustrious
friend the great Dean Swift used to say that history is made
by those who have a "strong style." Nobody, he would argue,
cares about "facts." The great Queen Elizabeth was actually
a puppet in the hands of William Cecil, but as she was com-
posed of brilliant colors and he of dull grays, she usurps his
rightful place in all the chronicles. Suetonius's Livia, in like
fashion, has blinded us to a hundred dreary senators and
generals, and, nearer to our own day, Louis XIV has emitted
gorgeous rays to distract the attention of posterity from the
grubbing ministers behind his gilded throne.

But it cannot be only that the more dramatic figures tend
to obscure the drones; it must be more than that. History is
a kind of rite; we read it in the faith that what went before
will help us to visualize what may come after, and even to
hope that what may come after will be for our betterment.
We do not care to dwell unduly on the casualties and costs of
wars; we prefer to emphasize what our Gallic cousins call
"*gloire*." We feel that *gloire* may be somehow the soul or
pulse of the nation, and if that be the case, what cost can be
too great?

Robert Harley, later Earl of Oxford and Mortimer, Henry
St. John, later Viscount Bolingbroke, and Abigail Hill, later

Baroness Masham, had very little to do with *gloire*. That may be why we have been so rapidly erased, or at least obscured, in the annals of this island's history. And I am beginning to persuade myself that Lord Hervey is right; that that is all the more reason I should set down my recollections.

Certainly, I have the time. My husband shoots all day and drinks all night. He is faithful enough to our *modus vivendi*; we rarely talk, but we also rarely quarrel. My son is busy with the farm across the way, he calls only on Sundays. I never entertain now, so the neighbors have ceased to invite us out. And then, too, when I was young, I used to dream that one day I should be a writer!

Yet I have the feeling, the odd feeling deep down inside me, that my words will be so much spray, evaporating on the weatherbeaten but stubbornly enduring monuments of John and Sarah Churchill.

2

I was one of four children, two boys and two girls, and I was born in London in the year 1680. So much has happened to our island since that day, eight years before good William and Mary stripped Mary's father, the proselytizing papist, James II, of his crown, and two decades before we were engaged, under her sister Anne, in an all-out war against the territorial ambitions of Louis XIV, that it is difficult for young people now to realize that at my birth we were ruled by a charming and amiable concealed Catholic, Charles II, who, unlike his fanatical younger brother and heir, believed in living and letting live where religion was concerned and in buying peace abroad and affluence at home by the simple expedient of taking bribes from the Sun King. Happy days!

My father, William Hill, was a successful merchant in the city, and my mother, born Jennings, was one of the many siblings of Sarah Churchill's father. We grew up in a handsome brick house in Chelsea in an atmosphere of ease and letters — my parents had a literary bent that I pride myself on having inherited — but all came to a sudden end in the nineties, when my poor father, after a series of reverses, became a bankrupt. The humiliation of poverty proved too much for his proud soul; he pined away and died, and my mother, who seemed to live only in him, soon followed. Alice and I and Jack and Frank, none of us yet twenty, had to fend for ourselves as best we could. There were uncles and aunts enough but none willing to support so large a brood, except with advice. I was finally placed in the household of a Lady Rivers in Kent.

The job was called a chambermaid's, but a laundress was what in fact I was. It was a lonely, cold house, and I had no friends and no opportunity to make any. I missed my sister and brothers bitterly, and my only diversion was a rare trip to London to see them. Alice was also a laundress, but the boys had done better, as boys in our situation always do. Frank was a page in the household of the Prince of Denmark, and Jack was in the army.

Queen Mary II had died, and her husband, the Prince of Orange, now William III, was reigning alone, as reluctantly legislated by Parliament when she had stipulated that she would accept the crown of her dethroned father, King James, only on the condition that her dour Dutch consort reign jointly with her. No one had thought he would survive her, but he had, and her sister had been deprived of her royal right for several years. Now, however, William's health was failing, and everybody looked forward to the day when the Princess of Denmark (as the heiress apparent was styled) should become a thoroughly English Queen Anne.

My parents had been of the Jacobite persuasion and used in private to toast poor old King James across the water, hounded from his throne, as my father put it, by his "pelican" daughters. But as Sarah Churchill, now Countess of Marlborough, was the intimate friend and supposed ruler of the allegedly passive Princess Anne, it seemed as if the Hills would have more to gain from the surviving pelican than from her exiled sire. Everyone expected the Marlboroughs to dominate the coming reign.

But could we poor Hills expect anything from a cousin so exalted? I had learned not to mention my relationship to Sarah to other members of Lady Rivers's household. On the one occasion that I had done so, it had been greeted with peals of laughter as a very good joke. And indeed how could anyone be expected to believe that a laundress was cousin-german to the second most important woman in England? There were times when even I could hardly believe it myself; when I was convinced that all the pleasure in the world to which I could ever look forward would be to read books in my time off and see my brother Jack advance in the army. For Jack was the one of us who was handsome enough and brave enough to succeed on his own. Perhaps one day he would marry an heiress who would allow me to be her housekeeper. Anyway, I could dream.

I shall never know what it was that put Sarah in mind of me, but when she was visiting in Penshurst Palace nearby, she drove over to call upon Lady Rivers. The old steward, who had always despised me as "too fine for my station," came with gaping mouth to the laundry to tell me to change my skirt and report to the drawing room.

"Milady Marlborough desires to speak with you, gal!"

When I arrived in the indicated chamber, discreetly garbed in gray, Lady Rivers, with some embarrassment, retired to leave me alone with this magnificent cousin whom I had never seen.

"I've come to take you away with me, Abigail Hill! I should

have done so before, had I known to what a sad position you had fallen. You shall be a member of my household, and if you are as well read as your sister tells me, you shall have a chance to become governess to my daughters."

"Then you have seen my sister Alice, Cousin?" I exclaimed in happy astonishment.

"She, too, is now a member of my household. Since last week. I have decided to do something about all the Hills!"

My heart almost burst at the vision of being reunited with Alice and freed from menial labor. At that moment I would have gladly died for Sarah Marlborough.

"Oh, madame! How can I ever thank you?"

"By being a good girl and a good governess," Sarah replied brusquely. She was evidently not one who cared for gushing. "And now I suggest you pack your things and come up to London with me. Lady Rivers has been so good as to agree to your leaving immediately."

Let me describe Sarah as she appeared to me then. Her skin was the purest alabaster, her eyes a flashing blue. Her nose, very regular, intensified one's sense of her force of character; her lips, sensuous and beautifully molded, were cherry red and the least bit petulant. Her hair was golden, and she held her head slightly to the side as she took you in — usually to find you wanting. Her voice was rich and warm, except when it rose to harshness or even stridency. She was, in brief, a magnificent creature, more like a goddess sent from Olympia on some Jovian mission than a mortal woman.

She seemed to forget me almost as soon as she had picked me up, but then she was the busiest creature in the world. Holywell House at St. Albans, to which I was now transported, was a bustle of activity, and Sarah was always on the rush between it and St. James's Palace, where she was reputed to run the Princess Anne's household as despotically as she did her own. I was soon found qualified to give lessons in

English history to the Ladies Mary and Anne Churchill, good-looking girls but spoiled and of imperious temper. It was not an easy task, but I found in time that I could manage it, and the servants, well aware of my relationship to their awesome mistress, treated me with respect. But best of all, I had my darling sister Alice, who acted as an assistant housekeeper, and we were allowed to invite our brothers to the house whenever they could come. Truly, I thought I had all I could ever want in life.

I did not come particularly to Sarah's attention again until I sickened with the dreaded smallpox. Let me solemnly record here that she saved my life. When none would go near me, the great lady herself sat by my bedside and held a bowl of ass's milk to my lips. I am told that on one occasion she even declined to leave me at the urgent summons of the Princess. Whatever else I may have to record in these pages of Sarah Churchill, let me set down here and now that she had the greatest courage and generosity. Had God given her less pride and stubbornness, she would have been as good a woman as she is a great one.

She sometimes came to the classroom to be sure that I was giving proper instruction in our national history. Having, with her husband and the Prince and Princess of Denmark, been actively on the side of Dutch William in the Glorious Revolution, she was an ardent supporter of the church and crown. But unlike the Princess Anne, who favored the Tory party, Sarah was a violent Whig who believed that England's great mission was to unite Europe against the aggrandizement of Louis XIV. She was probably looking forward already to the day when her husband, as commander-in-chief, would make Queen Anne as feared and respected in the Old and New Worlds as the Sun King himself had ever been.

I still had Jacobite leanings and said a quiet prayer at night for poor old King James, but it never would have occurred to me to create an issue with my splendid mistress, and I was perfectly willing to argue the cause of the Whigs to the girls, who didn't much listen to me anyway. I tried to preserve such small political integrity as I had by concentrating on the facts of constitutional history.

But now I must come to the master of the house — or perhaps the master of every house but his own. There is no man of our times about whom there have been more varying opinions than John Churchill. His worst enemies have gone so far as to accuse him of treason, driven by an avarice so fierce as to make him betray his own soldiers for silver. His lesser enemies qualify this position. No, they say, Marlborough never actually betrayed his country; he simply took money from the enemy without giving return. He was perfectly willing, according to these, to let King Louis pay for Blenheim Palace if King Louis had nothing better to do with his coins. But his partisans, of whom, despite everything that has happened, I remain one, insist hotly that he never took a penny that was not his legal due, and that, however rich he waxed in office, he would have been richer yet had his emoluments matched his merit.

All agree that he was a great soldier; to some, the greatest in our history. He never lost a battle, and he is reputed to have fought his engagements with supernal coolness and apparent ease. He would ride through Armageddon, unscathed and unsweating, in full control of the action, determined, impassive, even courteous! He seemed to have been born without fear and without temper; he moved his men in the battlefield like chess pieces at a game in his club.

And yet he was not a cold man, as this latter description may imply. When I first knew him, he was not yet the famous warrior that he later became; he was still kept back only by the military jealousy of King William. He spent much of his time at home, bearing his enforced idleness with a quiet dignity and treating his children, whom he adored, with a kindness and familiarity rare in fathers of that day. If he had a reputation for being stingy with the household purse — and I cannot deny that he deserved it — he made up for it by the grave, unfailing courtesy with which he treated his servants, down to the lowest scullery maid.

Everyone knows that he worshipped his wife. I cannot affirm it too strongly. He could not bear that she should suffer any pain, of mind or body. If she had even a mild headache, he would fret over her. It was strange to see this strong, silent man fussing about an obviously healthy spouse. It gave her a terrific power over him, for if he could not abide her discomfort, neither could he endure her wrath. The hero of Europe trembled before a shrew.

But they certainly made a handsome couple. His strong, erect figure and splendid marble features, his large, serene, unblinking brown eyes were the perfect set-off for her greater animation, her sharp high notes and roving, flashing gaze. Neither would have had to look twice to find a willing partner in adultery, but everyone, friend and foe, agreed that neither ever did. Yet Sarah constantly taxed her poor faithful man with infidelity, and it is a matter of history that she sent him off on the Blenheim campaign so wretched at her accusations that it was a wonder he could even think of the enemy, let alone annihilate them. But what my reader may find hardest of all to credit is that she once made a scene over me!

I used to see the then Earl of Marlborough almost daily at Holywell House. Like his wife, he sometimes came to watch his daughters at their lessons. But he never came when she was there. I suspect that he feared it might look as if he were interfering in a part of the household that was under her exclusive control. Milady was very strict in such matters. The daughters were *her* domain; the beloved young son and heir, Blandford, so soon, alas, to be lost to them, was his.

One morning I began my lesson with Ladies Mary and Anne in this fashion: "Today we shall discuss the succession to the throne. If King William were to die, Lady Anne, who would be King of England?"

"Nobody. The Princess Anne would be queen. Everyone knows that!"

"Indeed? And her husband, the Prince of Denmark, what would *he* become?"

"Nothing at all. He would continue to be nobody, just as he's always been."

"I think we should try to be more respectful about members of the royal family. But very well. Prince George would be simply the consort of a queen regnant. But can you tell me this, Lady Anne? Why was King William king? Was not the late Queen Mary also a queen regnant? Why was he not in the same position as the Prince of Denmark?"

Lady Anne now looked baffled. "I suppose because he made himself king. Is that right?"

"Papa made him king!" Lady Mary exclaimed.

"There was, it was true, a revolution, a glorious revolution," I interjected hastily, to mute so dangerous a topic. "And King James, the father of Princesses Mary and Anne, abandoned his kingdom and fled with his son to France. So it became necessary for Parliament to change the succession. And Parliament provided that the Princess Mary and her husband should reign jointly."

But Lady Mary was not inclined to concede such power to mere legislators. "You forget, Mistress Hill, that King William himself, like his wife, was a grandchild of Charles I. His mother was a Stuart princess!"

"Pardon me, Lady Mary, I do *not* forget that. It is perfectly true that he himself was next in line to the throne — *after* his wife and her sister. But it was Parliament that put him ahead of Anne. Otherwise, would Anne not have become queen when her sister died?"

"And a jolly good thing it would have been," Lady Anne retorted. "At least she has the *name* for a queen."

"Anne, you're such a silly!" her sister exclaimed. She turned on me sharply now. "I still think you're wrong, Mistress Hill. I don't care for King William, because he's always been horrid to Papa, but it was Papa, and not Parliament, that made him king!"

"Very well, Lady Mary. Let us examine your thesis. You maintain that King William is sovereign, independently of Parliament? Sovereign, that is, in his own right?"

"Certainly."

"Then if he were to marry now . . ."

"He's too old!" Mary interrupted. "And too ugly!"

"He's not yet fifty," I pointed out. "And as for his looks, I think it should not be difficult to find a willing bride for the King of England and Stadtholder of the United Provinces. So let me at least suppose His Majesty may marry and have a son. Who would succeed him?"

"Why, the son, I suppose."

"But that's just where I suggest you are wrong, Lady Mary. The Princess of Denmark would become queen, *de jure*, like her late sister."

Both girls at this condescended to show a mild surprise.

"That would be funny, wouldn't it?" Lady Anne surmised. "The King's sister-in-law coming ahead of a Prince of Wales!"

"And *now* do you see what I mean? Parliament has provided that Princess Anne shall take precedence over any issue of King William by a second marriage."

"I suppose that's only fair," Lady Mary commented. "Anne, after all, should have been queen since Mary died."

"Had Parliament not decided otherwise."

"I declare, Mistress Hill, you sound like a roundhead!"

"But she's right, girls, she's quite right! You have a smart teacher."

I jumped up to greet Lord Marlborough, who had just

entered the room. He walked slowly to where his daughters were sitting, smiling amicably, and ran his long fingers through Anne's curls.

"But, Papa, you must admit it's all nonsense!" Lady Mary retorted. "Parliament jumping in to provide that people should rule who have no proper blood claim!"

"Well, it happens I had something to do with that nonsense, Mary. It was the only way we could persuade the Princess of Orange to come over and take King James's place. Oh, she was adamant! Her William had to rule with her and succeed her, and that was that!"

"It seems to me it was a stiff price, Papa."

"We should all be bowing to the Bishop of Rome, my girl, if it hadn't been paid!"

"I don't know about that," Mary observed with a toss of her head. "But I *do* think it was a mistake to give all those horrid commoners the idea that they could fiddle with precedence. In the old days, if you had to get rid of a king you killed him. And kept on killing his heirs until you found the one you wanted!"

Lord Marlborough burst out laughing. "Is that your definition of the divine right of kings, Mary? I never heard it put quite that way before!"

Lady Mary jumped up to stamp an imperious foot. "Well, isn't it better to settle these matters with your peers and not go begging to burghers?"

"My, my, one would think that you issued from a long line of dukes and not a yesterday's earl!"

"Never mind, Papa. You *will* be a duke. And I don't forget we owe your peerage to King James and not to Dutch William."

"Are you a Jacobite then, lass?"

"Yes! And proud of it!"

"After all, Papa," exclaimed Lady Anne, with a sly wink at her sister, "isn't King James our uncle?"

"Your uncle, child? How is that?"

"Well, isn't he the father of Aunt Arabella's children? And doesn't that make him our uncle?"

The girls always treated their father in this familiar fashion. They did not hesitate to fling in his teeth that his sister had borne four bastards to James II. They knew that their mother ruled him, and even though they also knew that she would vociferously take his side in any intergenerational dispute, they still believed that a man who could be bested by one woman could be bested by another.

"I think that should conclude today's lesson," my lord exclaimed, and the girls hurried from the chamber, not because they had been dismissed, but because they were eager to leave class. Their father remained.

"Let me ask you something in private, Mistress Hill," he said now in a graver tone. "You have become a close observer of our household affairs. Would you be able to enlighten a worried husband as to the cause of his wife's distemper? For three days now Lady Marlborough has maintained a total silence at meals."

I confess to my reader that this simple question created one of the high emotional moments of my life. That this great, good man, this brave, handsome man, this friend of monarchs, should be reduced to asking a plain, red-nosed governess to help him find the cause of his domestic misery filled my heart to bursting.

"You are silent, Mistress Hill. Forgive me. I have embarrassed you."

"Oh, no, my lord! Not in the least. I think perhaps Lady Marlborough may be grieved that you seemed not to notice the anniversary of your first child's demise."

"Ah," he murmured softly. "So *that* is it. Poor little Henriette. Our first Henriette. What day, do you know, did the dear babe depart this world?"

"The seventeenth, sir."

"The seventeenth, just so. Three days ago. Thank you, Mistress Hill."

"If I may offer a suggestion, sir, why do you not bring Lady Marlborough a trinket that *would* have been ready on the seventeenth — had some wretched shopkeeper not botched the job?"

The grave eyes glittered. "Such as?"

"Well, you might have one of the miniatures of the child reset. And bring it to her tomorrow."

"Or this afternoon!" he exclaimed, jumping to his feet. "Bless you, Mistress Hill!"

And so began a curious relationship between my humble self and the great Earl. It became a silent pact between us that I should warn him of any reason I had to suspect that his spouse was displeased with him. Sometimes, of course, Sarah, who was not renowned for her diffidence, would announce in ringing tones to her husband — and to any of the household that happened to be within hearing — just what it was that had aroused her anger or suspicion. But at others she would retreat into sullen silence, and it was this that he dreaded most of all.

Other women were the most usual cause of Lady Marlborough's wrath. The Earl had only to be decently civil to a not ugly female, or simply to comment on her appearance, and his wife would flare. It was certainly no compliment to one of my sex to have been selected by Sarah to work in Holywell House!

"But I don't even remember *which* of the ladies at dinner was Mrs. Bartlett," Lord Marlborough might protest to me.

"You don't recall the redhead, my lord?"

"Oh, *that* one. My wife should be casting comedies at Drury Lane. She has an eye!"

But my reader may not be so much interested in the scraps

of conversation with which I attempted to keep the great man abreast of his wife's suspicious imaginings as in what was going on in *my* poor mind and heart. What did I feel when I found myself alone with Lord Marlborough, discussing a matter of the deepest personal concern to him?

I cannot say that I fell in love with him. I would not have dared to. *Can* one fall in love with a god? Of course, we read in mythologies that mortal women had such experiences and got turned into trees or cows because of the gods' attentions. I should have been quite happy to be turned into any bit of flora or fauna for the privilege of being for a single day the welcomed tenant of Lord Marlborough's heart, but I did not have the temerity to dream of such a thing. I knew that even as a young penniless officer he had been able to lure the Duchess of Cleveland, reigning beauty of her day, from the very bed of the "merry monarch" and sire upon her a babe that Charles II had reared as his own bastard. How could such a titan, even had he not given his whole heart to Sarah, cast a moment's glance at the likes of me?

Cousin Sarah's imagination, however, at least in this respect, was more copious than my own. She could step into her husband's shoes and fancy him sniffing after every female on the premises, including the poor governess. And then, in her own oddly democratic fashion, she would not scruple to use the same weapons against the governess that she would have used against another Duchess of Cleveland.

Sarah appeared one morning at the doorway of her daughters' classroom, erect and menacing, when her husband and I were having one of our talks.

"Will you leave us, Lord Marlborough!" she called out harshly. "You have no business that I wot of in the children's room!"

At which the bravest man in Europe rose and fled. Had he not been John Churchill, I might have used the term "scuttled." But always a tactician, he covered his retreat by leaving a morsel that the hungry predator could be counted on to devour before going after him.

"Well, Mistress Hill, is this how you repay my kindness? Is this your thanks for being saved from the pox?"

"I do not follow you, milady."

"What do you think you're doing with my husband, hussy? Do you want to find yourself pregnant and back in the streets?"

"Surely Your Ladyship doesn't accuse Lord Marlborough of seeking to debauch his wife's poor kin?"

The passionate injury in my tone gave even her a moment's pause, and she reappraised me now with a candid stare. "Well, you're no beauty, that's sure. But one can never tell what may strike a man's wayward fancy. King James ran after all the plainest faces in court. It was a known thing. Oh, I don't underestimate any female, Hill, when it comes to His Lordship! Tell me, then. What was he talking to you about?"

I decided that the truth was my only hope. I told my stony-faced, intently listening cousin the whole little story of her husband's concern and of my reassurances. As each episode that I related was recognizably accurate and as the only inference to be drawn was one highly flattering to herself, she was in the end somewhat mollified. But she was very definite in her resolve that these colloquies should be discontinued.

"I shall tell Lord Marlborough that he is to have no further private parlance with you. Look to it, girl! If I catch you again, out you go! For now, it's very well. I accept your story." She paused as she looked about at the scattered books and papers. "What a mess here! Clear it up, child. Clear it up!"

3

*M*y little talks with the Earl of Marlborough were forgiven
(if there was anything to forgive) but certainly not forgotten
by his watchful spouse. Sarah decided that I had better be re-
moved from temptation's way, but as she was always scru-
pulously fair (by her own exceedingly prejudiced lights), and
as she recognized that I had been guilty of no breach of duty
to her, she was determined that I should not suffer in salary
or position by my change. She decided to place me in the
household of the Princess of Denmark, and thus it was that I
became a bedchamberwoman to the future Queen of England.

I had no personal acquaintance with the Princess until
some time after her succession, which took place only a year
after my employment. Her household, of course, was a very
large one, and my position in it was lowly. In a less exalted
milieu I should have been considered a chambermaid, but

royalty sheds dignity over the most menial tasks. At Versailles, I have been told, a duke is not ashamed to bring a prince his chamber pot. Princess Anne was dressed, and her face and hands washed, by ladies of title. I saw her frequently, for I had regular duties to her wardrobe, but I never approached her person. She struck me as a solid, stolid, rather sullen-looking woman of middle age, very intent on the minutiae of her hourly existence, who never seemed to look beyond her immediate presence at the great world about her. Yet she had beautiful sad eyes that seemed to view her servants and courtiers with a faint apprehension, perhaps even a faint distrust.

It was enough for me to know that this woman had lost seventeen babies for my heart to forgive her any distaste that she may have manifested for the obsequious humanity that pressed so closely about her. Her husband, Prince George, would have been almost an attractive man had he been more lively and less stout. Unlike his wife, he was cordial to all, but one received the impression that he did not distinguish between the people at whom he grinned. He looked very much what he was reputed to be: a prince of small mind and kind heart who sought only to keep out of the way. His sole function had been to supply an heir to the throne, and he had been made painfully aware that he had failed, though presumably through no fault of his own.

The Princess and her late sister, Queen Mary, had quarreled bitterly over the former's stubborn refusal to dismiss Lady Marlborough, whom Queen Mary had hated, and this quarrel had led to a great reduction in the honors and perquisites of the Denmarks, and even to the withdrawal of their guards, but after Mary's death it had not been feasible for King William, sickly himself, to treat the heir apparent so contemptibly, and there had been some revival of their splendor. When the great day came, and Princess Anne found herself sovereign at last, there was no attempt by her household to disguise their rejoicing. In the course of the next year I found that I became as familiar with the palaces of Kensington, Windsor, Greenwich and Hampton Court as I had been with Holywell House or St. James's. But that has been the story of my life: either hovels or castles — with very little in between.

The court of the new Queen was a curious combination of magnificence and simplicity, of awesome regality and an almost middle-class plainness. On the one hand, Queen Anne was very particular about her prerogatives; she revived many ancient ceremonials, and seemed to relish the bowing and scraping and walking backward that Dutch William had affected to despise. She even restored the long-abandoned custom of touching those afflicted with the King's Evil, or scrofula, which disease was purported to vanish at the royal touch. But on the other hand, she could never quite overcome her native shyness, and she loved to hole up in the smallest and stuffiest suites that her vast palaces offered. Anyone having an audience in one of these and finding the Queen in a plain bedchamber robe, swathing her gouty hands in dirty bandages, would find it difficult to believe that he was in the presence of the poet Pope's "Great Anna, whom three realms obey." Yet, as soon as she spoke, her majesty of manner and sweet low voice helped to remove the initial impression. She was never a person to be taken for granted, as a number of statesmen learned to their sorrow.

Her coronation was the apotheosis of the Marlboroughs, now named Duke and Duchess. They seemed to carry all before them. John was appointed Captain-General of the allied armies in Flanders, in charge of the great coalition against Louis XIV, who had had the *hubris* to place his grandson on the throne of Spain as Philip V, and Sarah was named Mistress of the Robes and Groom of the Stole, in undisputed command of the royal household. As the first victories of the War of the Spanish Succession began to roll in upon us, it was commonly said that Sarah, who ruled both the Queen and the man who was defeating the armies of Europe's greatest King, had more power than any ruler in history. Indeed, I wondered if I had not left the greater service when I joined that of the Denmarks.

But I was content. I liked the anonymity of palaces. All I had needed was a job that I could handle and a quiet post from which to observe the passing scene. I asked no more. It was a relief to be away from the all-seeing gaze of Sarah, for, oddly enough, she spent little time at court. She seemed able to discharge her duties just as well from her own domiciles, and life in the royal palaces, except when there was a great court function, bored her. She made no pretense of her dislike of the Queen's warm chambers and was forever pushing open windows and fanning herself. She seemed to be growing increasingly impatient with her mistress's slowness and methodical nature. Seldom can two such close friends have been temperamentally so unlike. And certainly seldom has a royal favorite taken so little trouble to curry royal favor.

My first conversation with the Queen occurred when, in the illness of her trusted maid, Mrs. Danvers, I was delegated to bring her fresh bandages. It was on a long summer afternoon at Windsor, when she was having severe twinges of gout. As I was turning away, after spreading the bandages on the table by the armchair where majesty was sitting, I stiffened in surprise to hear the soft low voice address me by name.

"Hill, will you stay, please."

"What may I do for Your Majesty?"

"When you were engaged to serve in my household, do I not recall that the Duchess described you as her kinswoman?"

"Your Majesty's memory is correct."

"I like to think I know what goes on in court. Tell me, how are you related to the Duchess?"

"I have the honor to call her cousin, ma'am."

"But how close a cousin?"

"My mother was her father's sister."

"You mean your mother was a Miss Jennings?"

"Yes, ma'am."

"But then you and the Duchess are cousins-german! I had no idea it was so close a kinship."

"The Duchess does me great honor to recognize it at all, ma'am. My family were but poor folk."

"Well, I'm sure the Duchess is very kind. But cousins-german! Well, well, that does surprise me."

That was all that was said, but thereafter the Queen took more notice of me, addressing me by name and summoning me to her chair to bid me fetch this or that. Even the smallest notice of a menial arouses instant jealousy in a royal household, and I should have preferred my former obscurity had it not been for the encouragement of Mrs. Danvers, who adored the Queen with a selflessness rarely found in palaces.

"Never mind the others, Hill," she told me brusquely. "If Her Majesty likes your company, stick to Her Majesty."

The next step that I made in royal favor was when the Queen, who now professed a liking for my voice, asked me to read to her. When this proved satisfactory, I started to spend at least two hours a day with her. I read ministers' reports, ambassadors' letters, salutations from other sovereigns, novels and even plays. Sometimes the Queen would be so silent that I feared she had gone to sleep. Sometimes she had.

But my mistress and I did not enter into what I may be so bold as to designate a "relationship" until the day I made the suggestion that I might ease the pain in her hands. I had been reading from one of Sir John Vanbrugh's comedies when a little moan from the Queen indicated that I might as well stop. What I next uttered was probably the most important speech of my life. Yet I promise my reader that I had no purpose in mind but to assuage the sufferings of a woman who had been kind to me.

"May I respectfully offer a suggestion to Your Majesty? That might ease the pain?"

"By all means, my dear. Anything you could do in *that* line would be deeply appreciated."

"My father suffered as Your Majesty does. I discovered that if I had two basins, one with near-boiling water, and one with cold, and plunged his hand first in one and then the other, and then massaged it hard, he experienced some relief."

The Queen at once gave instructions for the fetching of these necessary things, and the treatment commenced. There was no talk now of majesty being touchable only by the fingers of peeresses; the poor suffering lady was only too anxious for my experiment. Happily it worked, and with the relief that I brought the Queen came further intimacy. Soon I was admitted to the bedchamber and allowed to rub the royal neck and back. My fingers were evidently as soothing as my voice, for I now became a kind of nurse as well as reader.

As soon as the royal entourage saw that I had established myself, all outward signs of jealousy ceased. I had now become a person to be reckoned with, to be cultivated rather than undercut. But the court must have been surprised at how little I changed. No honors were thrust upon me. The Queen accepted my ministrations placidly, with kind words and grateful smiles. But our conversations remained totally matter-of-fact. Any other woman with a good reading voice and a manipulative hand could have taken my place.

The reader may find it difficult to credit that it was the Duchess herself who paved the way for my further favor. She summoned me to her apartments at Windsor one morning and received me with her pleasantest smile, which, I may say, was a very pleasant one.

"I am delighted to hear, Cousin Abigail, of your success with the Queen! I have just been talking with Her Majesty, and I told her that I had depended on her unerring judgment of people to lead her in time to a recognition of your merits. I had been afraid, had I pushed you forward, that she would think I was doing a favor for a kinswoman. But now that she has found you, I can claim the credit of having put you in her way. You are just the person, my dear, to suit the Queen. You have cultivation, discretion and patience."

I listened, astonished. Was Sarah sincere? There could be no doubt of it. She was incapable of even a minor deceit. If she wanted to hide something, silence was the only way she could accomplish it, as her husband had learned to his pain. The explanation, as I soon made out, of her willingness to share with me any portion of her favor with the Queen was twofold. In the first place, it never occurred to her that she was sharing it. She conceived of my functions as so lowly and nurselike that I could never aspire to the high, free intellectual and spiritual friendship that existed between "Mrs. Morley" and "Mrs. Freeman." Was it even imaginable that a humble, plain bedchamberwoman could be a rival to the wife of the Captain-General? And secondly, she needed me. The Duchess of Marlborough needed Abigail Hill? How could that be?

Well, this was how it could be. The Duchess was bored with the Queen. She wanted to enjoy her great position and wield her power in the company of peers and statesmen and generals. She liked the busy world of London, where she could confer with the Whig leaders and preside at parties where the wit and fashion of the day convened. And, to do her justice, she missed her family, too; she wanted to spend more time with her handsome, bright children. Life in the small, stuffy chambers where the Queen liked to sit all day, playing cards or reminiscing about the past or giving instructions to gardeners, was anathema to her. There had even been times when I had wondered if frustration at court had not engendered an actual dislike in the Duchess for her mistress. I had once seen her take up a pair of the Queen's gloves that she thought were her own and then fling them down, muttering with a shudder: "Ugh! I almost put that woman's gloves on!" Of course, the Duchess, who, like many healthy persons, had a horror of illness, was probably thinking of the poor Queen's gouty hands, but some of her feeling about the ailment may have passed into her attitude toward the victim.

"You can be of some assistance to me, my dear," my cousin now continued. "You can be my eyes at court when I am away. Let me know at once if you see anyone gaining undue favor with Her Majesty!"

This promise I was able to give her with absolute sincerity, and we parted in the friendliest fashion.

I was soon made aware by the Queen's increased cordiality that the Duchess had in truth spoken highly of me. I believe that my mistress was sufficiently afraid of — or in awe of — the Duchess so that she hesitated to take any new intimate without her sanction. I do not mean to imply by this that the Queen was a weak woman — this memoir, if anything, should prove the contrary — but of two courses of action, one that pleased and one that displeased the Duchess, she preferred the former. She liked peace above all things, and peace with Sarah came at a certain price.

In our sessions now, when I rubbed my mistress's aching limbs, she would often talk to me about herself: her childhood, her lost infants, her happiness with the Prince. Sometimes this would take the form of a monologue, as it was not always easy for me, busy with my hands, to respond. The Queen liked to emphasize that I was not missing much in the married state; that it was at best a lottery in which she herself had been a rare winner. It was in one of her discourses on this subject that I made the astonishing discovery that she may have been as much a Jacobite as myself!

"Few of the Stuarts were happy in wedlock, Hill. My sister thought she was, but it was only at the price of giving in to her husband in everything, including letting him run her kingdom for her. And as for my poor stepmother, Mary of Modena, what a time she had with my unfaithful father! Even though she was young enough to be his daughter, and radiantly beautiful, too. When she was first told that she was to wed the heir presumptive to the throne of England, do you know what she said? She asked: 'Where is England?' That was how the Italians educated their princesses! Well, she knows where England is now, to her sorrow, poor dear, look-ing across the stormy Channel from her exile. I am no hypocrite, Hill, when I tell you that my heart sometimes smites me to recall what my sister and I did to King James and his wife. Maybe that is why neither of us had a child who lived. Maybe it is God's hand. Don't marry, Hill, if you can avoid it!"

"I can't say that I'm overwhelmed with offers, ma'am."

"Stay with me, child. I'll look after you."

I allowed myself a sentimental gesture at this, for I was becoming very fond of my mistress. I silently kissed her hand.

I should not give the impression that Queen Anne was al-ways indoors. She loved to hunt, not on horseback, which, with her figure and ailments would have been impossible, but wedged securely into a specially constructed chaise with two enormous wheels and a fast horse whose reins she handled herself. In this she could follow the hunt across coun-try with remarkable speed, to the great concern of the out-riders that tried to keep apace with her. She was very proud of this accomplishment, and when her ladies and bedchamber-women gathered on the terrace at Windsor to watch her de-parture, she would turn to wave her whip at us.

On the day that I saw her scan the row of faces on the parapet and smile when she recognized mine, I knew that my favor was special.

4

I had observed Mr. Robert Harley, one of the two Secretaries of State, as he went to and from the Queen's audience chamber. He was reputed to be a master politician and had been Speaker of the House of Commons, a zealous Tory who nonetheless sought accommodation with the Whigs. But my real reason for noting him was that he was my kinsman, a cousin-german of my father. He was not related, I might point out, to the Duchess, who was my mother's niece. I remembered seeing him at my parents' house in the days of our prosperity; he was considerably older, however, than I and would most likely not have remembered a plain, younger female cousin, particularly after her father's business failure had rendered any future intercourse with the Hills a source of probable pleas for help. I should never have presumed to remind Mr. Harley, in the day of his present greatness, that he had such a connection as a bedchamberwoman.

However, he *did* remember me. Of course, I was not so naïve as not to realize that any creature, however low, who has the smallest access to the sovereign is of interest to a minister. One had heard of the humble old Nanon, maid to Madame de Maintenon, who was cultivated by the greatest peers of France. But when Mr. Harley chose to notice me, he did it so charmingly that I could have forgiven him any motive.

He approached me after a service in the chapel of St. James's House and made a ceremonious little bow.

"I do not suppose Mistress Hill remembers an old cousin, but I am bold enough to claim her."

"Oh, Mr. Harley, I had not the courage to remind you! A member of the council!"

"The honor is all mine, my dear. The court goes to Windsor on Friday. I shall have rooms there, in the round tower. I expect sometimes of an evening to assemble a little group of congenial souls. We shall have good wine, and, I hope, good talk. It will be an escape from the rigors of court life. May I flatter myself with the hope that you will be one of us?"

"Oh, I should be only too happy!"

Mr. Harley fascinated me. Physically, I admit, he was not prepossessing. He was soft, pale and dumpy, with a round fat face, small, keen, blinking black eyes and a gleaming bald dome that I used to see in his soirées when he relaxed, wigless, smoking a long clay pipe. But he was invariably intelligent and quick-witted, and, unlike his friends, unlike most of the wits of the day, always humane. He would fan the air in mock dismay at the gibes and cuts of others; he would invoke the deity and roll his eyes to the ceiling at their "heathen Godlessness," as he liked to call it; but the person who had the last word was apt to be he.

Nor was all his conversation for his salon. He would draw me aside, as our friendship deepened, to show that he took a personal interest in my welfare. He could even be convincing about the reasons for his long neglect of the Hills.

"My own life has not been easy, my dear. I lost my beloved wife, and I had only a small property with which to support my children. And then politics kill a man! I have been so drenched in labor that I have had to neglect my nearest and dearest. And finally, when I got my head above the surface of civic duties and had at last a chance to look about to see what had become of my poor Hills, I heard that Milady Marlborough had taken you up. I thought you'd be all right then, and, besides, she has never had much of an opinion of your humble servant. But now that we've found each other again, Abigail, we must cleave together! There is nothing like blood. And we must get you married, my lass. Tush, tush, don't look at me that way! Of course we must. A fine girl like you! No, you needn't start protesting about dowries. There should be plenty of strapping lads about who'd be glad to marry a woman of sense and vision. Not to mention her being a cousin of the Duchess of Marlborough!"

I do not recall just who attended these small gatherings in Harley's drawing room in Windsor Tower — they were mostly new faces to me — but I do know that Henry St. John was always present, which must have been a compliment to Harley, in view of St. John's reputation for licentiousness with women and the paucity of opportunity for amorous encounters in those civilized, wine-sipping soirées. But I suppose St. John, who had just been created Secretary of War at Harley's instigation, could spare a few evenings from vice to dedicate them to the man he called "my master."

He was a young man for such prominence, still under thirty, and had looks to correspond to his reputation, being well-built, with handsome, if rather wolflike, features. He was almost comically Mr. Harley's opposite: emphatic, irreverent, salacious. To hear them arguing with each other — St. John, mocking, at times savage, and Harley, raising his fat fists in gestures of denial and gasping with dismay — was like watching a sparring dialogue in a Congreve comedy. But a sharper mind than mine might have pierced to the deeper division under the surface one and predicted an ultimate falling-out in this too-political friendship.

What fascinated (even if it at times appalled) me about the discussion in that narrow curving chamber, with its Dutch landscapes and the beautifully bound folios of Harley's collection that he had to have always strewn about even a temporary habitat, was their extreme freedom. Most of this atmosphere could be attributed to St. John, who seemed to glory in his lack of loyalties, but Harley, for all his asides to the Almighty ("May the good Lord forgive me!") and his playful deprecation of his "outrageous" disciple, nonetheless managed to convey an abundance of skepticism about the first principles of our church and constitution. I had never in my life, unless at my father's, when I was too young to recall, been the member of a group where the members contributed their thoughts and laughter to a common pool of truth, seeking it without regard for the rank, wealth, convictions or prejudices of the participants.

Strangest of all to me was the openness with which they discussed the progress of the war and the capacity of our military leaders. The great victory of Blenheim was then only a few months old, and the Duke of Marlborough was now the hero of Europe. Yet if my ears were correctly attuned, I heard St. John and Harley exchange anecdotes in which the Duke was said to be in correspondence not only with his nephew, the Duke of Berwick, a general in the French army, but with the Pretender himself! Nor did they hesitate to make mock of the Duke's greed.

St. John one night told this story about Marlborough's leaving White's Club after a gentlemen's dinner:

"His Grace claps his pockets and cries out that he has forgotten his purse! Will anyone be good enough to advance him the price of a chair? A dozen hands extend him coins; deprecatingly, he picks out the smallest. As soon as he goes we rush to the window and watch him passing up a line of waiting chairmen to take his pedestrian way home!"

A gentleman was then about to tell a story about the Duchess, when Harley raised a warning hand:

"None of that, my friend! We have Her Grace's kinswoman with us. I'll thank you to keep a civil tongue in your mouth."

"Oh, no, please, Mr. Harley!" I heard myself protest. "If I am to be a drag on the party, I'll take myself away."

And so, in a matter of weeks, I allowed myself to be put in a position where any spy of the Marlborough faction could have destroyed me with the Duchess. But I was having too good a time. I realized, more or less, that Mr. Harley, who had entirely neglected me in the days of my poverty, was noticing me now only because of my rumored intimacy with the Queen. But I had seen enough of court life at this point to suppose that this meant only that Mr. Harley was like any other courtier. What did I expect? To be loved for my red nose? I could consider myself fortunate that I had something that I could trade in return for membership in so charmed a circle.

One night, when Harley himself walked me back to my apartment, I felt compelled at the door to make him a confession.

"You've been very kind to me, sir, and I appreciate it deeply. I only regret there's nothing I can offer you in return."

His small eyes glittered with what, in the candlelight, I took to be amusement. "Do you imply that I expected something?"

"Well, in court isn't that usually the way?"

"Ah, I see! You thought that your wicked old cousin expected you to present some wily scheme for his advancement to Her Majesty? 'Make Harley a marquis, ma'am! Make him a duke!' "

"No, it was not that, sir. I assumed it would be something in the national interest. That is why I want you to know that the Queen never discusses anything of that sort with me. I am a kind of audience; that is all. She sometimes tells me stories while I rub her back."

Harley's laugh was so loud that I feared it would rouse the guards. "History is made up of less than that, my lass! But don't worry. Cousin Harley will ask you for nothing. You are welcome to my little evenings for yourself and yourself alone, my dear. If I ever come to you for a favor, it will be only that you tell Her Majesty that her faithful Secretary of State, who places her welfare far above his own, is waiting patiently in the corridor for the privilege of a few words!"

I went to bed, that night, happy and reassured. Little did I realize how vast was the privilege that my kinsman had just asked and that I had just granted. I had yet to learn that access to the person of Anne Stuart was the one true avenue to power. Needless to say, this was a lesson that Mr. Harley had long since conned.

5

I was happy now with my life at court. I loved the long quiet hours with the Queen that my impatient cousin had found so stiflingly boring. I found my mistress sound, even shrewd, and at times keenly amusing. She could not be hurried, and she did not like to be argued with, but I should never have had the temerity or presumption to attempt either. After all, I was comfortably housed and excellently fed, and, with my memories of a bleak past, enlivened only by the tantrums and tempers of the Churchill clan, I sought no better future. If I could only spend the rest of my days in this quiet service I asked no more, except, perhaps, to use my scrap of influence to help my brother Jack in his military career. The innocuous diversion, which only an idiot would not have savored, of living close to the center of power was all the entertainment I required.

It was inevitable that people should have accused me of meddling in politics and of seeking to influence the royal will. Certainly my cousin Sarah has openly indicted me with this often enough. But the curious fact — and one that she would never believe — is that I never did so until after her influence was entirely dead — exterminated by her own folly and passion. And my involvement then was only at the instigation of others, never on my own initiative. Left to myself I should not have attempted to convince the Queen of anything but that red wine and heavy meals were bad for her gout.

Yes, it is true; in those first years at court my ambition was entirely sated with the spectacle of rule. I had no wish to be aught than an observer. It gave me a pleasurable excitement to consider that, whereas the eyes of the world might turn to the glittering Captain-General in Flanders or to the great Whig lords at home or to the imperious Sarah roaming the empty corridors of her vast new palace at Woodstock to supervise and excoriate the builders, I, quiet little Abigail, known to the court as "Mrs. Still," was closer than any of them, as I rubbed the royal fingers with a hot rag, to the ineluctable force that controlled them all.

But what about marriage? Did I not want what every woman was supposed to want: a home, children, my own establishment? The answer is that I had thought of these things, yes, in my days of penury, but only as fantasies never to come true. I had neither a dowry nor the beauty to induce a gentleman to waive one, and I had too much pride to marry into a class where dowries were not required. The few men, mostly older, who had professed an interest in my person had made as little secret of their base intentions as I had of my scornful rejection of their advances. And now I had arrived at the age of seven and twenty, when a woman may be deemed to have resigned herself to the single life. The reader may not believe it when I say that there had never once been a mutual attraction between myself and a man, but it is true. Love for me had been only daydreams. I have already spoken of my sentiment for Lord Marlborough; it was as close to a "love affair" as I had ever come.

And so I proved an easy prey for Samuel Masham. It seemed to me a simple miracle that this handsome beau should feel, or even pretend to feel, an amorous inclination for red-nosed Abigail. All the fellow had to do was push, and down I went! He did not even have to convince me that his professed passion was genuine; he merely had to state it. He may even have winked as he did so; I was a disgrace to my sex.

I wish I could say in my own defense that I had been deceived. The sorry thing is that I saw him from the beginning as he was. The person who seduced me was myself.

But let me describe him. Although he was already showing signs of the fleshiness that has since overtaken him, he was still a fine physical specimen, thick-shouldered, stocky and well-coordinated. He had strong, regular features in a square, blunt face, but his eyes, large and gray-blue, had appeal and humor and even a hint of sensitivity. What attracted me most was my sense of the strong animal behind the mocking mincingness of his affectations. We were in an era famous for the exaggerated airs of its beaux. They liked to strut and saunter, showing off their fine muscles and limbs. It was their mode to underscore their masculine appeal by stressing its very opposite: by the elaborate ritual of raising snuff to the nostrils, or of contorting their features into theatrical expressions of woe and disgust, or of giggling like silly girls. Ours was a society in which it was considered a fine thing, in a duel of rapiers, to kill an opponent without drawing a bead of sweat.

I saw that Masham was trying his hardest to be this type, and this is not hindsight. I knew, after all, a good deal about him. He was a groom of Prince George and a captain who had never seen field service. He was the heir of a baronet with a small estate, which was no great thing in court. But he was personable, merry, up-to-date in his gossip and very determined to make a good impression. I see him now, as he first appeared to me, in yellow satin knee breeches with a skirted scarlet coat wired to make its ends flare away from his thighs, a ruffled lace shirt and high red heels. His hat was of black felt with a gold band, and his sword hilt was studded with aquamarines. He carried a muff, from which he occasionally extracted a perfume bottle, and he wore a full-bottomed wig with curls to cover what I later discovered was a fine crop of curly blond hair. Oh, yes, I took in every detail!

At Windsor, where members of the household in clement weather strolled at noon on the great terrace, Masham sometimes joined me. I thought little at first of his compliments, routine tributes to any person known to be in the least favored by royalty. But one morning I thought he seemed inclined to be more serious.

"Mistress Hill, I am afraid you find me but a light fellow."

"I find you charming to Her Majesty's women, Captain. His Royal Highness could ask no more of his grooms."

"You think it merely a duty?"

"Merely? What is better than duty handsomely performed?"

"I am obliged! But I assure you that it is far more than a duty."

"I am happy, anyway, that you do not find it an onerous one, sir."

I still thought we were engaged only in Windsor persiflage. But now he sounded a more personal note. "We have something in common that you do not suspect, Mistress Hill. A love of letters. You have, I know, a taste for fine writing. And a high style of your own."

Had he told me that my nose was white, I could not have been more surprised. I liked to flatter myself that my correspondence could boast an occasional happy turn of phrase.

"Where have you seen any samples of my poor efforts, Captain?"

"I have the honor of Mr. Harley's friendship. He is your kinsman, I believe?"

"He is good enough not to deny the bedchamberwoman."

"He is proud enough to acknowledge the Queen's friend! Mr. Harley took the liberty of reading me a letter that you wrote him when the court was at Greenwich. It contained a charming description of the Lord Mayor's barge. Mr. Addison could scarcely have improved on it."

I was charmed. I had been particularly proud of that letter. "I blush that Mr. Harley should have made so much of my humble prose. Are you a writer, Captain?"

"I am writing a tragedy."

"Indeed! Is it in couplets?"

"I prefer not to be the prisoner of rhyme. My thoughts disdain fetters. But, of course, I use the heroic meter."

I repressed a smile at the grandeur of his disdain. Mr. Dryden had not deemed rhyme so limiting. "May I ask the subject of your tragedy?"

"I have taken it from the French master, Corneille. It is an adaptation of his tragedy *Pulchérie*. Do you recall the story? No? It is about a Byzantine empress, a virgin, who, having succeeded to the throne in early middle age upon the decease of her younger brother, is urged by her council to marry. Not wishing to share the imperium with any man, she rejects a young prince, whom she adores, for an aged general. Her condition is that the marriage shall not be consummated."

There was a pause as I considered this bizarre plot. "But would that not defeat the purpose of the council? Did they not seek an heir to the throne?"

"Apparently not. The council was less concerned with an heir than with having a man to guide the sovereign in affairs of state."

"But why the condition, then? Would not even a nominal husband have had the same right to guide his spouse?"

"I presume not, under Byzantine law. At any rate, Pulchérie feels that she will be stronger as a virgin monarch."

"I see. It's most interesting. Do you believe it will be a subject of interest to a London audience?"

"Not precisely. My tragedy would appeal to a more select group. Perhaps in a performance here. I see it as a delicate compliment to the Queen."

I stared. "Surely you are not suggesting, sir, that Her Majesty's marriage contains a parallel?"

Masham laughed loudly, even rather crudely. I was destined to become much acquainted with that laugh. "Hardly, after all those stillborn babes! I could be sent to the Tower for such a suggestion. No, I am reflecting on the fact that the Queen likes to preserve the rule entirely to herself, a resolution that the Prince honors and understands. We all know that Her Majesty welcomes comparisons to the great Elizabeth. It is only politically that I consider her a virgin queen."

This, I was to discover, was typical of Masham. He was totally unable to conceive that other persons might view things differently from the way he did. Fortunately, he had so many little projects in his mind that they were rarely executed. *Pulchérie* never grew beyond a single act.

"Do you contemplate a career as a man of letters?" I inquired politely.

"Perhaps not quite a career. A gentleman couldn't very well do that, could he? But statesmen and diplomats today are inclined to the pen. A taste for letters has become very much the thing. Your cousin Mr. Harley collects rare books. Mr. Prior is accounted a first-class poet. Sir Thomas Hanmer is supposed to be editing Will Shakespeare. Mr. Addison and Mr. Steele are received in the greatest houses."

"And Monsieur Racine gave up the stage to become King Louis's historiographer."

"Precisely. You are well informed. Happily for Racine, he did not live to be obliged to record the recent victories of our Captain-General. But to return to a humbler scribe, would you condescend to read some pages from my tragedy and favor me with your words of wisdom?"

"I should be only too pleased."

And so our more intimate acquaintance began. We met daily now, sometimes on the terrace, but more often in Mr. Harley's apartments, where Masham was a regular guest. I never did see any pages of the famous tragedy, for after a bit he seemed to forget all about it. If my reader is surprised that Masham should have been so welcome in Harley's intellectual circle, let me explain that he provided his host with a perfect foil. Masham's laugh was loud, constant and infectious, and he could be pleasantly ribald when he was not quite adequately witty. I was titillated but ashamed when Harley joked about my obvious interest in his "protégé." But he soon waxed more serious.

"What do you say to our young friend as a suitor, Abbie?" he asked me one afternoon on the terrace, where we watched the return of the royal hunt. "He admires you. That is obvious to all."

"Oh, that's just badinage," I said, reddening.

Harley pursed his lips into a small knot and raised his eyebrows. "It's difficult for a woman to tell, isn't it? How they go on, these fellows! But suppose he meant it?"

I felt my mouth go dry. I need not hide from these pages that Samuel Masham's body had already become a magnet to me. Even when I found him foolish, almost ridiculous, I was giddy in his proximity. His perfume and his male odor simply undid me. Impatiently now, I tried to shake off the image.

"What could it come to?"

"Why not to a marriage?"

"To a servant? You dream, Mr. Harley."

"To a royal servant? To a cousin of a secretary of state? To a cousin by marriage of the Captain-General?"

"Without a penny to her name?"

"The Queen would give you something."

"It would never do."

"Think about it, my dear! Just think about it."

Needless to say, I did. In my daydreams, following this colloquy, I was already in bed with Mr. Masham. I did not for a minute believe that he loved me; I knew that he wanted only to be close to Mr. Harley and to the Queen for the purpose of promoting his own career. He meant to subjugate me, to sleep with me, if he could, certainly not to marry me. He had perfectly divined that I was attracted to him; there was an air of near-insolence now in the freedom of his flattery.

"You have reduced me to a sorry state, Mistress Hill! I, who used to be the diversion, even the terror, of half the maids at court, now languish in corners, pouting till my sun appears. But my sun seems to shine on everyone."

"Or on none."

"Spare me a beam! One beam just for myself, enchantress! Give the rest, if you must, to the garish world."

"Captain, I must go to the Queen now."

"Could you not spare a beggar a coin?"

"A coin?"

"A kiss!"

"A kiss! Really, Captain, do you think me so rich as to spare beggars gold pieces?"

"On the cheek, merely, then."

"Captain, I shall be late!"

"And I sent to the Tower. Unless . . ."

"There! You took it. I did not give it."

This sort of nonsense was froth to him, but it was horribly upsetting to me. I was in such a constant fever now that I could hardly concentrate on my duties, and only my awareness that any loss in royal favor would be followed by the immediate loss of my lover enabled me to keep my mind in any sort of order.

It was a second and more intimate conversation with Mr. Harley that proved my undoing. The next time that the Secretary approached me on the subject of Masham, I told him flatly that I did not propose to be used as a pawn in any man's career.

"His pawn? But, dear girl, you'd be his queen!"

"I don't care, Mr. Harley! I do not wish to be made sport of." And then, to both our astonishments, I began to sob. "It is wretched for a woman to be told a lot of things by a man that he does not mean!"

"What does Masham not mean?"

"All his love and what-not. All his burning and dying and sighing. All my being the sun and moon and such trash!"

"And what makes you think there is no passion behind his words?"

"Because I'm ugly, Mr. Harley! A man like Masham could love only a beautiful woman."

Harley's little eyes became even smaller as he puckered his face into his worldly-wise expression.

"Let me tell you something, my dear. I think you are wise enough to take it in good spirit. You must learn that women know very little about men. You take it for granted that a handsome fellow must have a beautiful girl. That may be true of some of them. But not of all. And certainly not of Masham. Look at your dogs and cats. Do the males care about beauty? They do not even care about age. A mastiff will run after any old bitch in heat. You will forgive an elder cousin his plain language. Masham would have the same rapture with you that he would have with a beauty such as Milady Somerset."

I was shocked, but not angered, by his crudeness. There

was something of Pandarus in the way the idea of Masham's brutal and indiscriminate masculinity seemed to tickle him. I recalled now that he was always placing his hand on Masham's sleeve or tapping him on the shoulder. But the effect of his words was still devastating. The notion that in submitting to my would-be lover I might be giving as well as receiving pleasure undermined the last pillar of the wobbly pier of my defenses.

Thus it happened that Masham achieved access to my chamber and person. But the reader may still wonder, despite my preamble, why, at the age of twenty-seven, with a reputation for modesty and good character, and having viewed the antics of the great world from a privileged position, I should have succumbed quite so swiftly to the advances of so typical a seducer.

I have stated my sexual inexperience, my plainness and my resignation to the prospect of a life in which I had no hope of enjoying the rites of love. These were elements in my undoing, but they would not in themselves have overcome my character. What did this, I am convinced, was the habit of daydreaming, of erotic fantasizing, which had occupied so many of my idle thoughts during the long hours alone in my chamber, or strolling in the royal gardens, or simply sitting by the Queen while she read or played cards or dozed. It was the fact that Masham happened to fit so neatly into these that enabled him to prevail in the game that I was at all times perfectly aware he was playing.

And there was yet another factor. I loved plays, both tragedies and comedies, and Mr. Congreve was my particular passion. I was fascinated by his heroes, those superb, foppish peacocks, so magnificently virile despite their airs and drawls, who strutted before the hens, declaiming their "worship" with images of "flames" and "sighs" and "deaths." Their love was like their spread tails, a dazzle of color intended to hypnotize the poor hens, who had only their bit of wit to protect them. The female of the species had two choices in the stage world of Congreve, both humiliating: to yield at the altar and become, soon enough, a betrayed spouse, or to yield without sanction of the altar and become a whore.

It was the game of the male to entice his victim into the second alternative. Marriage, unless it was a question of dowry, was only a last resort. The peculiar fascination of the game, to my eyes, was that it was played with such brutal candor. The words of passion were intended to inflame, not to fool. Women were like the captives of ancient Rome, flung into the arena with weapons not quite equal to the fangs and claws of the beasts loosed upon them, with the choice of being killed or surviving only to be made to fight again. The gallant who took a pinch of snuff as he drawled to Amarinta that he was dying in her displeasure was really telling her that she was already a whore in heart who might as well become one in fact. And in my dreams and fantasies I would be seized by the degrading urge to give in, to become a whore, *his* whore, to be trampled upon, used and flung away on the trash heap, where I belonged.

And, indeed, my triumphant lover entered into my fantasy quite as if it had been reality. He treated me as the French monarch might have treated a conquered province in Germany. He never even suggested that marriage was a possible consequence of his possession. I got my just deserts.

6

*M*y cousin the Duchess used to say that there were women who conceived if a man so much as kissed their fingertips. It seemed I was one of these. After our marriage Masham kept me constantly pregnant, and the brief intimacy that preceded our lawful union proved equally fruitful. I had my first dizzy spells within days after I first succumbed to him.

I awoke immediately from my feverish daydreams. I was not sure that I had not been mad. What was horribly clear, at any rate, was that I had placed myself on the road to certain disgrace, that I had destroyed in one moment the safe and comfortable port that I had miraculously reached after a lifetime of desolation. And for what? A great love? Even at my headiest moment I had not regarded my feeling for Masham in that light. A great pleasure? Well, I have never made love with any other man, but if his performance was the equivalent of Marc Antony's, or of any of the fabled amorists of history, the delights of the body have been sadly overrated. And I do not care if one day Masham *does* read these lines.

My strongest reaction was shame, shame that I had been party to such a sham proceeding, shame of my low excitement at the prospect of my own debasement, shame at the folly with which I had turned from my beneficent mistress to give myself to the first rake that solicited me. On the morning when I first realized my condition, I turned away sharply from its odiously smiling cause. Masham had been waiting for me outside the Queen's door.

"Keep your hands to yourself, sir!" I hissed when he tried to put his arm around me.

"Hey, now, Abbie, what has come over you?"

"That I've been a fool once doesn't mean I must stay one!"

And I swept off, to leave him gaping.

Harley, from whom nothing at court could be long concealed, deduced at once what had happened from Masham's account of my behavior. We were now at Hampton Court, and he bade me visit him in his apartments, which were in the old Wolsey section of the palace, small dark rooms with massive chests, red hangings and linen-fold paneling. I stood by a narrow window, looking bleakly down on the courtyard while he, in his bantering tone, reproached me.

"That you, dear coz, of all people, you, our admired 'Mrs. Still,' you, the very embodiment of prudence and decorum, should prove a wanton! You make me feel that I have been a sadly behind-time Laertes. I should have warned you not to open your chaste treasure to our captain's 'unmastered importunity.' "

"Laertes! It is of another of Master Shakespeare's counsellors that *you* put me in mind!"

"Do you mean Cressida's uncle, you hussy?" Harley exploded into a fit of laughs mingled with rasping coughs. "But, my dear girl, I wasn't trying to bring you to Masham's bed! On the contrary, I expected you to be a pinnacle of virtue!

The worst you could say of me was that I was a marriage broker."

"Marriage! That's something you can forget about now."

"What makes you say so?"

"Because Mr. Masham will not marry a whore!"

"Ah, my dear." Harley's tone was kinder now as he took in my tears. "Mr. Masham is still serious about marriage. Only his price has gone up."

"His price?"

"He expects the Queen to make him a peer now."

"He won't ask her *that*!" I cried in dismay.

"No. But I shall."

"Oh, Mr. Harley, the shame of it! I can't endure it."

"Tush, tush, child. The Queen's a Stuart; never forget that. Think of her father and uncle! I have arranged more difficult matters with her. Masham will not get all he wants, but he will get something. And I shall be surprised if we do not have a royal godmother at your son's christening! Cheer up, lass."

"But I don't want to marry Mr. Masham!"

Harley wagged a finger at me. "You should have thought of that before you let him tumble you."

What could I say? Of course I was going to marry Masham if there was any way it could be brought about. The alternative was to be dismissed from court and give birth to my baby in the street. Even Harley would not have given me shelter had I spurned his advice. And as for the Duchess — I knew only too well how *she* would treat me. She had cut her husband's own sister for the same offense, and Arabella Churchill had had a king to sire her bastard!

"I suggest that you mend your fences with Masham," Harley continued in a more practical tone. "You have him much upset. A word, a smile, and all will be well. In the meanwhile I'll speak to the Queen. The less time that we lose, the better."

It was agreed that I should be in the adjoining chamber when Harley spoke privately to my mistress, and that the door would be left ajar. At the appropriate moment he would call my name, and I would hurry in to fling myself on my knees before her. My heart, when the terrible time came, was beating so rapidly that I could hardly distinguish the first words of the interview. It did not make matters easier for me that when Her Majesty's voice became at last intelligible, I recognized the note of stiffness that signalized her stubborn moods.

"You wish to speak to me about a favor for Mrs. Hill, Mr. Harley? Is it not a household matter? Should you not address yourself to Mrs. Danvers? Or even the Duchess?"

"Perhaps, ma'am, I have allowed my concern for my kinswoman to carry me beyond the bounds of a strict etiquette. But I venture to observe that even in the court of a sovereign as greatly beloved as yourself, the ardor of Mrs. Hill's devotion to Your Majesty stands out."

"The girl is fond of me, I do believe."

"Ah, ma'am, she lives for you!"

The Queen's voice at this seemed to relent. "What is it that you seek for Hill, Mr. Harley?"

"Something that will put her future on a more stable basis, ma'am."

"More stable? Can she be more secure than with my favor?" The edge had returned to my mistress's tone. "Or do you, Mr. Harley, like those ravens in the court of the Elector of Hanover, look forward to an early demise of the crown?"

"Heaven forbid, ma'am! May they perish while you still hold your scepter high! I was merely referring to the establishment that every maiden may wish for herself, even one so happily situated as Mrs. Hill. I mean marriage, ma'am."

"Is Mrs. Hill aware that you are speaking for her in this connection?"

"She is, ma'am."

"Then I suppose it is Mr. Masham you have in mind."

"Nothing escapes Your Majesty's eye!"

"So *this* is what you call Hill's living for me!" But the Queen's tone was not unfriendly. "Well, I have no objection to Mr. Masham. So long as he will not take Hill away from court. She is quite indispensable to me. But as Mr. Masham is a member of the Prince's household, I presume there will be no question of any such removal. Very well, Mr. Harley. You may tell Mr. Masham that he has my permission to offer himself to Hill."

The silence that ensued conveyed to me some sense of Harley's embarrassment.

"Mr. Masham has ventured to suggest that under the circumstances Your Majesty might deign to consider a promotion for him."

"Under *what* circumstances?"

"My cousin, ma'am, is a dowerless maiden. Nor can she point to any great distinction in family."

"She can point to *you*, Mr. Harley. Not to mention the Duchess."

"That is true, ma'am. But her father was in trade. Mr. Masham, as the heir of a baronet, might look higher."

"What must he have to take her?"

I knew that the pause that followed meant that Harley had dropped all idea of a peerage. "Would you consider making him a brigadier, ma'am?"

"To wed a woman of my bedchamber? Mr. Harley, are you serious?"

"Could you make him a colonel, then?"

"A colonel! And I thought you were talking about a gift of a hundred pounds or the rangership of a royal park. No, Mr. Harley, your candidate holds himself far too dear. I think poor Hill must forgo any dreams of wedded bliss."

I saw what was coming and wanted to forestall it. Anything

would have been better at that moment than the truth! But Harley pressed inexorably on.

"I fear, ma'am, there is another aspect to the case."

"And what is that?"

"I crave Your Majesty's indulgence."

"Speak on, man!"

"My cousin is an excellent and virtuous woman. But there are some ardent young couples today, ma'am, who anticipate the privileges of matrimony without awaiting publication of the banns."

I could picture, with a sinking heart, the drawing-down of my mistress's lips.

"Are you suggesting that Hill and Masham have been such a couple?"

"I'm afraid so, ma'am."

"And with the usual results? Is the girl breeding?"

In the silence I could picture Harley's reluctant nod of assent.

"The strumpet!" the Queen cried in a suddenly sharp tone that brought my hands to my ears. "What will the Duchess say? How can I tell her that Hill has been debauched in my service? That she has been wantoning with this lewd fellow under my very nose?"

Almost before I knew what I was doing, I had rushed into the chamber and thrown myself at the Queen's feet.

"Oh, ma'am, forgive me! Do not cast me off! Had I had the blessing of your kindness and example in my younger years, I should never have so misconducted myself. I have never loved any man as I have loved Your Majesty! I was tricked into submission, ma'am. I did not know what men were!"

"Mistress Hill!" Harley exclaimed sharply. "You forget yourself. Leave this presence."

"No, Mr. Harley," the Queen intervened in a gentler tone. "I think it is you who had better go. Leave me with Hill."

When I was alone with the Queen, she said nothing. She simply sat and looked down at the floor with half-closed eyes. This did not surprise me. I knew her moods. I had learned that when she went into one of her silences, it was not only futile but unwise to try to elicit the faintest response, either of voice or gesture. But I had also learned that she could listen at such times, and that if I did not pester her with questions, she might even follow my argument.

"Your Majesty has told me of a young maid of honor who was sent without father or mother across the water to serve in a strange land. And about what happened to her when she was courted by a handsome prince who professed only honorable intentions."

I then had the boldness to relate to the Queen the story of her own mother. It was a daring proceeding, but I was in a desperate situation. I recited, as if I were reading from a book, how the young Anne Hyde had been sent to Holland to be a maid of honor to the Princess Royal of England, newly married to the Prince of Orange, and how she had there been wooed by the Princess's brother, James, Duke of York, who, like her other brother, the still unrestored King Charles, had found time heavy in exile and pretty maids of honor a pleasant distraction.

The Queen did not so much as nod or stir as I went through the whole sorry tale of her mother's seduction, the secret marriage that had followed the discovery of her pregnancy, the fury of Lord Clarendon, more loyal to the crown than to his own progeny, who had implored Charles II, now back on his throne, to annul the marriage and fling his daughter in the Tower, and, finally, the benign mercy of the King, who had insisted that his backsliding brother should publicly re-wed the mother of his child and make her officially Duchess of York.

"All I have ventured to hope is that Your Majesty might show some of the same compassion that filled the breast of her royal uncle. I have always believed that Your Majesty resembled him more than she did the other Stuarts." I was being obvious in my flattery, for it was known that the Queen liked to have attributed to herself any part of the famed charm and wit of Charles II, but I had to take the risk. "It was perhaps because King Charles had himself prevailed over so many of our sex that he had learned to tolerate our frailty."

"Which my father never did!" the Queen exclaimed suddenly, and I was at once silent. She went on now, in a reflective monotone:

"And yet he had as many mistresses as my uncle. But my father's were always ugly. Uncle Charles used to say that he must have chosen them as a penance. Oh, Hill, I fear my father was a hard man! I used to be appalled at the tortures that he allowed the Scots to inflict on their dissenters, when we lived in the north. And as for the horrors that followed the suppression of poor Monmouth's rebellion . . . well, they were beyond words. Some people think it must be great to be a queen, but I think you, Hill, have a sense of what pain and soreness it can bring. Why did they want my father to marry a princess and not a commoner? I'll tell you why! Because if a monarch is not to be bowed to the ground with the sadness of his task — all the horrible wars, like this one we're now in, and all the bloody executions — he must have royal blood, which means coldness to human agony. Yes, it is true! It is my Hyde blood that is my undoing, that makes me wring my hands over the war and the woes of man, like Uncle Charles, whom people so carelessly called the 'merry monarch.'" The Queen paused now and then announced suddenly: "We will see Mr. Masham, Hill. Send for him."

"Right now, ma'am?"

"Right now. You need a husband, my girl!"

When Masham had been summoned, and he and I were standing together before the Queen's chair, I had to admire his composure. As I had no idea what tack my mistress would take, he could not have, either. And yet he had the confidence to contemplate majesty with smiling eyes!

"Hill has informed me of her condition, Mr. Masham," the Queen began gravely. "It is not one in which I care to find the women of my bedchamber. Are you prepared to do the honorable thing?"

"With the greatest of pleasure, ma'am! And may I express my deepest regret that the fruit of our mutual ardor, if I may take the liberty of putting it so, should have caused any concern to Your Majesty's peace of mind?"

I found this both vulgar and impudent, but the Queen did not seem to mind. "All's well that ends well, Mr. Masham," she said complacently. "The ceremony had better be secret so that gossips will not be able to calculate the months. We shall attend as witness."

I fell upon my knees. Masham merely bowed low.

"May I inquire, ma'am, if Mr. Harley has spoken in my behalf?" he asked.

"He has." Masham did not know the meaning of those lowered eyelids, or he would not have persisted.

"And has Your Majesty seen fit to consider his petition with any favor?"

"No, Mr. Masham, I have not. Your conduct to Mrs. Hill may be deemed a fault that marriage will rectify. There is no occasion for reward, beyond the happy possession of a worthy spouse."

Masham's smile became even brighter. "Perhaps Your Majesty has not been apprised of my circumstances. I am in no position, alas, to afford a wife."

"You should have considered that before you became so intimate with Mrs. Hill, sir. Future promotion will depend on how you treat her."

"And if I decline the honor, ma'am?"

"Then I am afraid we shall be deprived of the pleasure of

seeing you at court. There are islands, however, in the New World where my officers can usefully serve."

Could the great Queen Elizabeth have put it better? Masham, to do him justice, took his licking like a man.

"Your Majesty's favor is all the dowry I shall need," he said, with another deep bow. "May we have Your Majesty's permission to marry tomorrow? If it will not inconvenience Your Majesty to attend a ceremony at so short a notice?"

"That will do very well, Mr. Masham. We observe that you are a man of good sense. So you may profit by one more piece of good counsel. We do not wish to see lugubrious countenances in our presence. If Mrs. Hill's mood is a happy one, your fortunes will prosper. You have a vested interest in the contentedness of your spouse, sir!"

The royal nod indicated that the audience was over, and Masham could only bow and depart. His sharp quick glance at me indicated that I was to accompany him, but I decided that the time had come to make abundantly clear to my future life companion just where my first duty lay and would continue to lie. I remained with my mistress.

✣

When I went the next morning to Harley's apartments I found my "betrothed" there before me. He took not the slightest notice of me as I entered, but continued to pace up and down the chamber as he excitedly talked. Harley, relaxed and bald, without his wig, was sitting by the fire, puffing at his long clay pipe and smiling in the amiable fashion with which he was wont to meet the troubles of others. He silently waved a hand toward the chair that I should take, as if I were a latecomer to an amusing play.

"I'm tied up like a cow for a rutting bull!" Masham was almost shouting. "I'm trussed and garroted! All that little jade has to do is dab an ink patch on her temple and tell

Great Anna that I smote her. And then, thank you very much, poor Sam here will be dispatched to some hellhole of a Carib isle to sweat out his days overseeing a troop of blackamoors. Was ever a man so had? Why, if the new Mistress Masham so much as sighs in the royal presence, she will be asked: 'What has the fiend been doing to my little dove?' "

"You're like Bertram in *All's Well*," Harley observed with equanimity, and I remembered that the Queen herself had referred to this title of Mr. Shakespeare's.

"I'm telling you I bleed to death, and you talk of Bertram! Who's Bertram? Some literary character, I suppose. Do you *live* in books, Harley?"

"He's the hero of one of Mr. Shakespeare's comedies," Harley replied, unruffled. "Helena is the poor cousin who loves him, but who cannot look so high. However, when she cures the King of France of his fistula, she is rewarded by being allowed her pick of the royal knights for a husband. She chooses Bertram, of course, but he protests to the King that she is not his equal."

"And the King lets him off? It's easy to see he didn't have a *queen* to deal with!"

"On the contrary, the King commands him to marry her. Bertram can avoid his fate only by stealing off to the wars." Here Harley winked at me. "We shall have Sam in Flanders yet, Abigail."

"I may well come to it! Think of it! To marry a chambermaid! And why? Has *she* cured the Queen of a fistula?"

"She's cured her of something just as bad: ennui. Sam, you're making a great fuss over nothing. If your name is ever in the history books, it will be as Abigail's husband. When will you learn, my lad, that in the game of power it's not title that counts, but proximity to the royal ear?"

"But the Queen doesn't govern. *You* should know that. Doesn't everyone say she's putty in the hands of her ministers?"

Masham came over to Harley now and straddled a chair, leaning over its back to face his interlocutor. I reflected sourly what a poor creature I was about to marry. His present indignation was as feigned as his erstwhile ardor; he had no passions at all, only a mild acquisitiveness. If Harley could convince him that I was an asset in disguise, he might very well prove an amicable if uninteresting spouse. But, oh, my dear mistress, my afflicted, worried sovereign, with what greatness of heart had she intervened to save her servant! As my mind rocked back and forth between Masham and my liege lady, I wondered if I should ever love any person, even the babe beginning in me, as I was now learning to love Queen Anne.

"Many bigger men than you have made that mistake about Anne Stuart," Harley expounded patiently. "Take it from me that, in the last ditch, she has a will of iron. She can be pushed just so far, kicked just so hard, and then, bang, you find that your foot is shattered. There are many great peers, many great Whig lords, but don't forget it is *she* who prorogues or dissolves Parliament and *she* who picks and discharges her ministers. She could reduce the great Marlborough to a simple ensign tomorrow. She could . . ."

"Don't forget what happened to her father!"

"And don't you talk treason, my friend! King James used his power stupidly. But he had it to misuse; that's my point. His daughter isn't going to make that mistake. In fact, she isn't going to make any mistakes. She bides her time. Bide along with your wife-to-be, Sam, and you may yet see great things."

"Great things for whom?"

"Great things for all of us."

"Give me one instance."

"Come, doubting Thomas, you must learn some faith! But, anyway, how else can you play your hand? The Queen wants the marriage; it would be folly to refuse her. If you perform it in a sullen fashion, you will lose all credit with her. Therefore be cheerful! Act as though it were the highest honor in the land to marry a woman of her bedchamber, and . . ."

"And?"

"And who knows? You may yet be a peer."

Masham turned and bowed to me. "Greetings, Lady Masham!" he exclaimed mockingly.

But at least he was smiling now; I was to wed, it seemed, an easygoing man. Love? Of course he did not love me. He would never love any woman. After all, did I love him? I might deem myself fortunate to have a father for my unborn child. I think it was at that moment that I had my first premonition of what my matrimonial life would be: Masham would keep me always pregnant to show the world that I belonged to him. And that as soon as I began to swell he would desert my bed for any other that was offered. As Harley had said, he was one of those males that can mate at any time with any female. There are worse husbands. At least he has never beaten me, and if he ever reads these pages, it will be too late.

7

Masham and I were married in Dr. Arbuthnot's apartments in St. James's Palace in the presence of the good doctor and his wife, my sister Alice (whom I had now established in the royal household), Mrs. Danvers and the Queen. None of us wore a wedding garment, and the ceremony took place in an almost conspiratorial silence and haste. Dean Thompson, who officiated, started reading the service as soon as my mistress, assisted by her trusty companion, Danvers, had hobbled through the doorway to take her seat in the armchair by the improvised altar. The moment he had delivered the benediction, the Queen rose, embraced me and took her leave. Masham, mollified by the royal presence, was an almost passionate lover that night.

The next day my duties were resumed in normal fashion, and the Queen made no comment on what had happened.

My husband and I continued to dwell apart, but as the Prince's apartments adjoined the Queen's, visitations were easily arranged and, at least in the first months of my pregnancy, were frequent. Nobody need have learned of the marriage until my condition betrayed it, had not the Queen's wedding gift of two hundred pounds showed up on the household accounts and attracted the immediate attention of the Duchess of Marlborough, as dutiful to the royal finances as she was negligent of the royal person.

I was informed of this by the Queen herself. She seemed upset when I came to her chamber that morning and pulled me close to her when I knelt to tie her slipper.

"The Duchess knows about your wedding. She found my gift in the accounts and challenged me about it. You should have heard her! I might have been a housemaid caught with her hand in the till. When I told her what it was for, she really burst out. Why had you not come to her first? I told her I had advised you to."

This was not true, but was it up to me to contradict the Queen? I nodded.

"Shall I go to her, ma'am?"

"Yes. Right now, I think. But aren't you scared, child?"

"How can I be scared when I married with Your Majesty's blessing? What can the Duchess do to me?"

"She can make a great racket."

"I shall survive it."

I curtsied and took my leave. But my heart failed me for a moment when I faced the Duchess, magnificent in blue, seated on a divan of white damask in her apartment. Her tone was loud and harsh as she fixed her lustrous eyes on me.

"Well, Mistress Abigail! Is this the way you treat your nearest kin? By letting your cousin Sarah, who rescued you from penury and an early grave, learn that you have taken a husband by reading of the Queen's gift?"

"I crave your pardon, Cousin. I wanted you to be the first to know . . ."

"And not the last, miss!"

"I wanted you to be the first, but I lacked the courage to intrude my little news on the attention of one who must bear the world on her shoulders. And when the deed was done, I was so terrified at not having told you, I resolved to keep it a secret!"

The Duchess appeared to consider my excuse. For a moment I almost hoped that she would accept it. But this hope blew away with her next response.

"Surely you know me better than that. Have you ever seen me neglect the least of my duties because of greater responsibilities?"

"I dared not think that I was one of your duties, Duchess."

"You are my kin. Did you think I might disapprove your choice?"

"I thought it possible."

"It was more than possible. I *do* disapprove it. Very much. Was Masham a man to wed the cousin of Lord Marlborough's wife?"

"I hadn't presumed so to think of myself."

"Well, you may be sure Masham had!" The Duchess's laugh was half snort, half cackle. "You may be sure he saw the Captain-General behind the red nose of the bedchamber-woman!"

I flushed. Even from her I had not been prepared for such rudeness. "Mr. Masham is a worthy man," I murmured.

"A worthy man to smirk at the Prince's jokes. And to skip to open a door for his betters!"

"Cousin, you are severe!"

"Do you think I don't know the man? You've picked an ass!"

I had to take a deep breath to guard my temper. "It was not in my sphere to look higher. Mr. Masham is all I want."

"Well, even if your aim is as lowly as you say, I'm surprised that *his* is. What made him take you so poor? Are you pregnant?"

"And if I were," I retorted, frankly angry now, "how would that have aided me? Had I a father to protect my honor and march a man to the altar? Had I anyone but a cousin who insults and reviles me?"

"You had your bully of a brother Jack. He's quick enough to quarrel. I don't suppose your gallant would have relished that. Masham's sword, I daresay, is more for show than use."

It was now that I made my mistake. It was not like me to be indiscreet, but, really, her arrogance was more than flesh and blood could bear! That she, married to the greatest soldier in Europe, should jeer at my husband's courage! Were *no* insects too small for her treading heels?

"Do you really think, Duchess," I demanded in a cooler tone, "that if mine had been the forced match you suppose, the Queen would have honored us with her presence?"

Well, if I was an insect, at least I had stung! Sarah made no effort to conceal her astonishment. "The Queen was there? The Queen went to your wedding!"

"There were only six persons present. It was at Dr. Arbuthnot's apartments at Saint James's."

"And the Queen went without letting me know! Are you trying to tell me, Mistress Masham, that you have supplanted me in Her Majesty's affections?"

In my embarrassment and confusion I failed to sense the heavy sarcasm of her tone. "Oh, I'm sure Her Majesty will always be kind to you!" I exclaimed.

"Kind to me!" The Duchess rose, dark of countenance. For a few moments she seemed actually unable to speak.

"Get out of this chamber!" she shouted at last, and I fled before the tempest.

8

A week later I was seated by the Queen in her drawing room at Hampton Court. Her armchair had been pulled up before the bay window so that she had a full view of the great fountain, which was in full play. Never had I been more conscious of the contrast between the monarch and the woman. My poor mistress was having bad twinges of gout. One of her feet rested on a footstool, tied up in a poultice, and she clasped a dirty damp bandage in her right hand. Her robe was loose and stained in front from saliva that she had just coughed up, and her face was red and mottled. It was almost impossible to keep her clean. But on the ceiling, over her chair, she was painted, erect, majestic, on a throne floating amid clouds, adored by the Graces, attended by the Muses, a bright sword held upright in one hand, the scales of justice dangling from the other, while at her feet a cornucopia spilled out the riches of her realms.

"The Duchess is very wrathful," she said in her flat tone. "She wants me to dismiss you. I asked what you had done. She said you had been guilty of the basest ingratitude. That you owed her the smock on your back; nay, your very life."

"It is true, ma'am."

"Then you *have* been ungrateful?"

"While I was employed by the Duchess, I served her loyally."

I knew better than to get ahead of the Queen. In her good time she would ask me all the questions that she wished answered. Royalties are not like other persons. They are naturally suspicious, even of those whom they most wish to trust. From childhood they have been surrounded by masks.

"What about after your employment had ceased?"

"I was then in the service of Your Majesty. Does the Duchess suggest that my first duty was still to her?"

The Queen grunted. "She says you deserted her for me."

"It was she who placed me in Your Majesty's household. Did she mean my first duty still to be to her?"

"She claims that having proved a deserter once, you may prove so again. That you are not to be trusted."

"Assuming me to be treacherous, to whom could I betray the Queen of England?"

"To France. To my brother at St. Germain."

When the Duchess threw stones, she certainly picked large ones! But I wondered if even she would have made so reckless an accusation. Could it have been the Queen's idea? I shuddered, recalling as a child being dragged by my brother Jack to see a man hanged and quartered for treason. I had screamed and closed my eyes and put my hands over my ears, but not before I had witnessed horrors that I still think of when I wake up in the early morning.

"I have no friends in the court of St. Germain, ma'am. The Duchess has a sister there."

The Queen was silent for several moments. "I told her I was going to keep you," she said at last.

"Bless you, ma'am!"

She looked at me in her steady, sad way. When I say there was something cowlike in that gaze, it sounds impossibly impudent. Yet there it was, the hurt, suspicious, resigned look.

"You don't want to leave me, child?"

"Forgive me, ma'am." I leaned over to press my lips upon her gouty hand. "I love Your Majesty. I love Your Majesty, God forgive me, more than I love my husband. More even than I loved my poor father."

It was true, and the Queen believed it. That was the whole secret of the rise of Abigail Hill. The Queen had become my life. People will say it is impossible to love a queen entirely for herself, that the desire to approach a monarch is too strong an urge not to pre-empt a good part of what might otherwise have been a natural affection. And then it may be argued that Queen Anne lacked the personality that would have inspired such devotion had she been born in a humbler sphere. These things may be valid, yet the love that was inspired in me, as a subject or a servant or even a nurse, was still a complete and abiding love. However it came, whencesoever it came, it was the force of my existence.

"I shall *not* give in to the Duchess," the Queen observed now. "I shall not give in, no matter how she rants and raves."

"Surely, once Your Majesty has made clear her decision not to discharge me, there need be no further discussion of the matter."

The Queen's eyebrows rose. "You know your former mistress better than *that*, child. She does not style herself Mrs. Freeman for nothing."

"But Your Majesty can cease to be Mrs. Morley! She can be Mrs. Freeman's sovereign again. Until the Duchess decides to accept Your Majesty's decision!"

The Queen sighed. "Mrs. Freeman is a wonderful woman. She has done a great deal for me. But she has used me sorely in recent years. I think no one who has seen us together could deny that." Her voice rose suddenly to a near wail. "You can't know, no one can know, what my life has been!"

It was the sign that she wanted to talk, and I bowed my head to listen.

"You see before you Anne, the Queen, and you are awed by my power. You think I have only to speak, to raise my hand, and it will be done as I say. You are too young to re-member how swiftly my father lost his throne. One day he was reviewing his cheering troops on a white charger, doffing his plumed hat to my beautiful stepmother as she gazed down on him from her balcony at Whitehall, the undisputed master of three realms! And the next, he was fleeing in dis-guise, dropping the great seal overboard in the Thames. But even at that he was more fortunate than *his* father. He did not have to step out of the banquet hall of his palace to a scaffold on a cold winter morning and lay his sainted head on the block!"

"Oh, ma'am, don't even think of it!"

"I think of it constantly, child. The Stuarts' heads were never secure. Think of my grandsire's grandmother, the Queen of Scots! People talk of the divine right of kings! A divine right to decapitation; that's what it sometimes seems to me. And if God *were* on the side of the Stuarts, would He be on mine? Am I not sitting on a throne that belongs right-fully to another? To my own little brother over the water whose birth I slandered? For Mary and I claimed he was a foundling, you know. Oh, yes, we did! We told people that my father's Queen was not breeding, that a child had been smuggled into the palace in a warming pan. Will God forgive *that* if it is not true?"

"Even if he be the true Prince," I murmured, tempted to

agree, but fearful that perhaps I was being tested, "his religion must bar him from the throne."

"And who is to decide that?" my mistress retorted in a petulant tone. "Parliament? Who gave *them* the right? If they have taken upon themselves to regulate the succession, to bar this person or that person, have we not an electoral crown?"

"But surely, ma'am, they bar only Catholics."

"And suppose those Catholics are converted? Should not their claims revive? Suppose, when my brother comes of age, he elects to return to the Church of England? Should he not succeed me?"

"Yes!" I could not help crying out my jubilant response.

"So you *are* a Jacobite after all," the Queen said, with a nod of satisfaction. "That was another thing the Duchess told me. But I don't mind. I *loathe* the idea of a Hanoverian succession! Why should I leave my beautiful realms to a fat, stupid German who can't speak two words of our language?" Indignation had now suddenly aroused the Queen, and there was a flash of fire in her dull eyes. "Consider this, Hill. They eliminate my father's issue by my stepmother, as Roman Catholics. Very well. Who is next? The issue of my aunt Henriette, the poor poisoned Duchess of Orléans. These include all the Savoys. Out, as Romans! Very well. So they turn next to the issue of my great-aunt, the Queen of Bohemia, daughter of James I. There are forty-odd of these, including all the Condés. Out, as Romans! Until they come to my great-aunt's youngest daughter, the Electress of Hanover, and there at last they stop. Is it well? The Electress and her son are not Romans, true, but neither are they Church of England! So why, having gone so far, not go one step further? Who is the next heir? The Duke of Somerset! A fine man, and English, too, the first of the whole motley lot who is, and a devout member of the Church of England, to boot. What perversity is it that makes Parliament, having romped all over Europe in search of a successor to my poor self, stop just short of one of their own body?"

"Perhaps because the Marlboroughs don't want a Tory."

"You *have* kept your eyes open," the Queen said approvingly. "And now do you see why even a queen has to be afraid of the Churchills? They toppled my father! They convinced me that he would have brought all England back to Rome. But how do I know that now? And how do I know, if the Duchess does not have her way, that she will not summon the Captain-General back from Europe to clap me in the Tower?"

I felt suddenly giddy at the idea that it was the Queen of England who was actually saying this to me! Could it be thus that history was made? Could the great Duke proclaim himself Lord Protector, like Cromwell? Could he drag my poor gouty mistress, with her soiled bandages, to the scaffold and have her head struck off? Surely, I could imagine what short shrift would be made of the wretched bedchamberwoman who had precipitated the crisis! But then I shook my head. The Queen was indulging in fantasy.

"I don't suppose I should be worth such a rumpus, ma'am."

"No, you wouldn't, Hill," Her Majesty agreed. "If the Duchess really wanted to dethrone me, she would pick a greater issue than my bedchamberwoman. Which is why it is safe to resist her, about you, anyway. And I shall. But, oh, Hill, I did love that woman!" There were sudden tears in the Queen's eyes. "Nobody can be a more wonderful friend than Mrs. Freeman when she *is* wonderful. But she must always have things her own way. Was ever a friend used as I have been used?"

I was silent. It was not my function to traduce the Duchess. I could only marvel that Sarah should have used her great power so recklessly.

"I tell the Duchess that she has no time for me these days," the Queen continued sadly. "That she is understandably occupied with her children and the building of Blenheim. I don't criticize her for that. But how can she not understand that I need someone who is more available? She has offered to spend more time at court. She has even offered to take over some of your functions. But, oh, Hill, can you imagine having your back rubbed by the Duchess? Why, she would break my spine!"

The Queen relapsed now into silence, and I sat silently beside her, wondering at the difference between this harassed and kindly woman and the figure of Britannia on the ceiling above.

9

The next two years of my life were trying ones. I was almost
constantly pregnant, having two daughters born within eleven
months of each other, and I was the target of the unremitting
campaign of hatred launched by the Duchess. She did not, it
is true, subject me to any personal abuse or attack; when our
paths crossed in court, she simply looked through me. But the
poor Queen was continually harried by her appeals that I be
dismissed, and there was no member of the cabinet or the
royal circle whose ear did not ring with her lurid tales of my
ingratitude, promiscuity and probable treason. When so much
mud was flung, some of it was bound to stick, particularly
where the assailant was the second lady of the realm.

Of course, a good deal of what Sarah did was self-defeating.
She gravely underrated not only the Queen's innate stubbornness, but the extent to which the violence of her slander

reinforced it. Sarah had none of her husband's high sagacity as a fighter; she did not understand the danger of making her opponent desperate. She could not comprehend that a wise commander will always provide terms of surrender that are not too flagrantly humiliating. She could not see why, if she was right — and it never crossed her mind that she was not — the enemy should not throw down his weapons, fall upon his knees, make a full confession of his sins and bless the victor for chastising him! I began to realize, before the battle was half over, that my silence might be worth her violence and that the Queen might as much appreciate my never mentioning Sarah as she objected to Sarah's seeming never to mention anything but me.

My relations with my husband in this period were the best that we were ever to have. Later, as I shall have occasion to relate, his demands for wealth and promotion were to give me considerable trouble, but in these two years there was a suspension of the tension between us. He was apprehensive of what Sarah might accomplish against me in the battle, but, powerless to intervene, he was at least sensitive enough to perceive that he might do well to provide me with the moral encouragement of an unquarrelsome home. I saw him little in the daytime, but I could expect his company at night, except when my figure was too swollen.

The Duchess was with the Queen a good deal more than had been her wont before her discovery of my favor. To avoid embarrassing confrontations, it was arranged that I should never be present when she was. Of course, she imagined that I was always hovering in the wings, and she would frequently raise her voice to make a slur on my character. But I had no desire to hear her insults, and as the Queen was naturally uncommunicative, I was more ignorant than the rest of the court of the progress of Sarah's campaign. I was even the last to hear of her biggest strike: the removal of

Harley as a secretary of state. He, as well as I, had become her target since he had deserted the war party to work for a negotiated peace.

On one of my visits to Harley's chambers I noted what I called his "heroism in the face of injustice" expression. I knew enough of my kinsman to learn that he assumed airs of tranquillity and high resolution in direct proportion to the rising success of his opponents.

"They have arrested my confidential clerk," he told me blandly.

"Greg? Poor little Greg?" I had a vision of a mousy fellow who used to vanish into the recesses of the chamber whenever I called on his chief. "Whatever for?"

"The great Sarah is in luck this time. Apparently 'poor little Greg' is neither so poor nor so little as we suspected. He got hold of a letter from the Queen to the Emperor, requesting the transfer of Prince Eugène to the Spanish front, and sent it to Versailles! Fortunately, at least for the national interest, it was intercepted."

"But, Harley, that's treason!"

"And we know the penalty for treason. Greg is now in the Tower. How long he had been in King Louis's pay, I have no idea. The question for me is: What will he say on the rack? Whom will he try to incriminate?"

"You take it very calmly."

"I take it the only way I *can* take it, in full confidence of my own innocence. The worst they can say of me is that I was careless to trust such a man."

"But he may invent anything under torture!"

"He may indeed. I am in God's hands. But even at best, I shall have to quit the ministry. I have already sent my resignation to the Queen. The Whigs can hardly allow a Tory to remain in the council after a blunder of this magnitude."

"You will leave me alone at court to face the Duchess?" I cried in dismay.

"I shall be right behind you, Abigail! In almost daily conference. You will be my eyes and ears at court. It is not only the Duchess we will be fighting. It is the whole brutal, senseless war!"

Had the Duchess taken advantage of this moment, when she had stripped me of my principal support, who knows whether she might not have carried the day? My poor mistress was beginning to weary of the battle; she might have given me up to achieve at least domestic peace. But I verily believe that Sarah was at times a madwoman.

"Poor little Greg" was put through the appalling tortures that were still used to extract the names of co-conspirators from those wretches accused of high treason. Yet for some arcane reason no amount of racking could induce him to incriminate Harley. His agony was a vivid example to me of the stakes for which the Whigs were playing. One did not lightly drop out of a race such as I was engaged in. It was like one of those sports contests which we had learned about from Spanish accounts of the ancient Mexicans, where the losing team were massacred for the delectation of the mob.

There were so many ways that the Duchess could have prevailed! It almost seemed as if she enjoyed the sport of heightening her hurdles. Had she appealed to her old intimacy with "Mrs. Morley," admitting and apologizing for her neglect of the Queen in recent years; had she dropped her political arguments and invective and concentrated on the bond between two bereaved mothers of such promising sons as Blandford and Gloucester; had she sounded the note of solidarity that must have existed between two women who had risked their very necks in the Glorious Revolution, who knows if the bedchamberwoman, having no share in either the nostalgia or the glory, might not have been dismissed? But no, Sarah had to have my head, so to speak, as a matter of *right*. The Queen must not only give me up; she must admit she had been wrong!

The Duchess now went so far as to suggest to the Queen that her relationship with me was an unnatural one. One day my mistress, grim-faced, handed me a letter to read.

"I don't know if your stomach's strong enough, Masham, to digest that!"

It would have been a shocking epistle for any woman to write to another, let alone to her sovereign. The Duchess did not hesitate to stoop to quotations from scurrilous ballads hawked about the public houses of London. She assailed the Queen's "strange and unaccountable passion" for a woman that she, Sarah, had taken "out of a garret." And she concluded on this note: "Nor can I think that having no inclination for any but of one's own sex is enough to maintain such a character as I wish may still be yours!"

I knelt down before the Queen and kissed her hand.

"Send me away, ma'am dear," I begged in tears. "Let me go far from the court. Do not keep me here to bracket Your Majesty's name with such filth."

"I shan't let you go, Masham. There can be no idea of that now. Play the harpsichord! Play me something that will take away the stench of that epistle!"

✣

The next time that I saw my magnificent cousin was when she burst in on the Queen to announce the Duke's triumph at Oudenarde.

"I don't know if Your Majesty will consider my news worthy of interrupting so delightful a tête-à-tête. But word has just been received that my husband has won another glorious victory!"

The Queen gave her a level stare. "Do we know the casualties?"

"Not the figures, no. My lord writes that they were heavy. Heavier, I am glad to say, for the enemy than for us. Your Majesty's victories are not bought for nothing."

The Queen's hands flew to her temples. "Oh, when will all this terrible bloodshed cease!"

"Is *that* Your Majesty's reaction to a victory that will make her the first sovereign of Europe?"

"First sovereign of a graveyard," my mistress muttered in a voice that only I could hear. But when the Duchess asked her to repeat it, she waved her away.

This was bad enough, but worse was to come.

The victory procession to the thanksgiving service at St. Paul's Cathedral was to start from St. James's Palace, where I, though more than eight months pregnant, was still on duty. As the Duchess was very much present in all the preparations, including the dressing of the Queen — it seemed more her jubilee, indeed, than her mistress's — I had been excused. I was surprised, therefore, when an usher scratched on my door to tell me that I was wanted in the royal presence immediately. When I came to the Queen's bedchamber, the other ladies, evidently in obedience to an earlier command, withdrew. My mistress, looking tired and worried in her great royal ermine robe, was seated before a table on which some of the crown jewels in open cases were arrayed.

"Masham, look at these!" she exclaimed petulantly. "Look at what the Duchess expects me to wear! Three diamond bracelets! Four ruby clasps! The emerald and sapphire earrings! And the pearl choker! Why, I shan't be able to move!"

It was true that the stones were enormous. Lying placid on black velvet, they seemed fatuously confident of their great worth. They emitted a dull, possessing gleam. The Queen continued:

"I feel as if I were going to be pulled along behind the Duchess's chariot, as in a Roman triumph! Like some great gilded idol captured from the Barbarians! It is all *her* day, *her* victory. Well, let her go to the cathedral alone, then. Why should I be there?"

"Why may Your Majesty not select her own jewels? Why need she wear any, if she does not choose?"

"Because the Duchess will say I am snubbing the Captain-General!"

"Is it a snub to show respect for our dead and wounded? Are *they* not to be remembered?"

"They should be, indeed. Heaven knows there are enough of the poor lads. Crushed under the Marlboroughs' wheels!"

My eye traveled rapidly over the objects on the table. I picked up a small crucified Christ, Byzantine, of cracked yellow marble, a beautiful thing and the only one without a single gem to adorn it. A plain necklace of gold wire was attached to it.

"May I place this around Your Majesty's neck?"

I had barely accomplished this when the Duchess swept in, seething in scarlet, alight with diamonds. She stared through me as if I had been a void.

"Has Your Majesty made her selection? The procession is ready to start." She paused as she took in the cross. "Surely, ma'am, you're not going to wear that ugly figure?"

"If Our Lord made an ugly figure on the cross, Duchess, it was to redeem us."

"Well, of course, I meant no irreverence. I suppose it won't be noticed under the necklaces. May I assist Your Majesty? There is very little time."

"I am wearing no other ornaments."

"You mean you're going to the cathedral like that?"

"I am wearing no other ornaments."

"But Your Majesty will spoil the day if you go so plain. What will people think? It will be a scandal!"

"I am wearing no other ornaments."

The Duchess shot a quick glance at me. Then she changed her tack. "My dear Mrs. Morley, you have allowed yourself to be poorly advised. Believe your trusted Mrs. Freeman. A glorious victory requires a glorious presence! You should not let down the men who have defeated your foes."

"I am not letting down the men who have died to defeat them. Let us go, Duchess."

My kinswoman at this seemed to lose the last vestige of her self-possession. She stamped her foot.

"You have been listening to that low creature! You have been taking *her* advice as to what you should wear to my husband's service! How can any woman, let alone a sovereign, be so blind, ma'am? Don't you see that Masham's only object is to demean me and Lord Marlborough so that she can wrap the crown of England in her chambermaid's apron? Oh, that I could only make you *see* what she is! But no, you are too besotted with that plain brown thing; you are too enchanted with your hussy . . ."

"Duchess!" The Queen interrupted her with a gasp of horror. "You forget Masham's condition!"

"Forget it? How could I, with her big stomach stuck in my face? Can't you at least send her to her chamber? Or do you want her to ride with you to the cathedral so that all your kingdom can see for what base company you abandon their hero's wife!"

The doors burst open, and we saw the red uniforms of the household guard lined up along the corridor. The court chamberlain, in a gold uniform, approached, to bow low to the Queen. Through the open windows on the stairwell below we could hear the cheering of the crowd outside.

"I must ask you, Duchess, not to make any further reference to Masham. It is hardly her fault that . . ."

"Be quiet, ma'am!"

It was the Duchess who said that! And in a voice that carried to the corridor! The Queen, half-dazed, moved forward as the guards presented arms, and the Duchess followed her to the stairwell. The procession to the cathedral had begun.

I learned later that Sarah continued her angry protestations in the royal carriage and did not cease until the Queen had actually started down the aisle at St. Paul's. But I had staggered back to my chamber in a fainting condition. That night I gave birth to my second daughter.

10

Masham had not attempted to conceal his disappointment that our second child was also a girl. It did not seem to me a matter of very grave consequence that we should still lack an heir for a baronetcy that he had still not inherited. I was always to love my children equally, even after I had sons. What concerned me principally was avoiding another pregnancy, and I exaggerated to my too-amorous spouse the ailments that had followed my delivery. It did not improve his temper.

"Harley thinks you're indulging yourself," he reproved me. I was sitting up in bed in the handsome bedchamber of the apartments at Kensington that the Queen had provided for us and which were now the permanent home for our babes. Masham had spent the night with his father in Kent and had just arrived back in town. "He says you are leaving the Queen to the mercy of the Duchess while you loll in bed and drink chocolate!"

"I wish Harley had had to bear two children in under a year!"

"Well, I've got a bit of news that should get you up, my girl. The Duke of Marlborough himself is demanding that the Queen dismiss you."

"What are you saying?" I cried.

Masham, delighted to have made such an effect, handed me a letter from Harley. As I read it I seemed to feel my heart contract; my shoulders twitched, as with a sudden chill. Harley had written that the Earl of Sunderland was telling everyone that his father-in-law, the Duke, had suggested to the Queen that he could not continue his burdensome duties abroad if she persisted in keeping as her intimate advisor a creature of Harley's who was known to be inimical to his conduct of the war!

"I shall send the Queen my resignation today!" I cried, throwing my head back on the pillow. When Masham tried to console me, alarmed at the violence of my reaction, I waved him away. Only when I screamed at him did he finally abandon the chamber.

How could I fight the whole world? While only the Duchess and her clique pursued me, I could find the courage to resist, exhausted and harassed as I was. There was enough spite in her to pump spirit into the most abject opponent. Sarah would kick her toppled victim until in sheer agony and despair he rose to fight back. But the Duke, the glorious Duke? He who, with the coolness of Hannibal and the courage of Alexander, risked his life daily to lead his battalions against the mightiest army of Europe! And who had proved that a mightier existed, forged, trained and commanded by his own genius! How could I live with the hideous idea, even if it were false as hell, that a bedchamberwoman with a red nose was impeding the greatest soldier in English history from marching to Versailles itself to dictate peace to old Louis, cowering in his gilded saloon!

No, I had to find a way out, to beg my poor mistress to try to live without me, to take my babes and fly to my father-in-law, if he would take me in. I should have to placate Masham somehow, give him a son if possible, or, if he were implacable, throw myself on the Duchess's mercy and plead for a pittance in return for my promised absence from court!

I do not know how long I twisted and turned in my bed, but it seemed to me it was dark when the door opened again and my husband's head reappeared.

"Go away!" I cried. "I'm sick!"

"I've brought a friend."

"I don't want to see anyone!"

"Oh, I think you'll want to see this one."

"Who is it?"

"Well, it's not the Duchess!" This, to a silly laugh.

"I suppose it's Harley."

And in came my old friend, all smiles, both hands outstretched. There was no resisting him. He called for little Abigail and was shrill in his exclamations that never had there been a more beautiful baby. Only when he had finished his rhapsodies did he turn to business.

"What's this I hear about you deserting the cause, Abigail? Will you give up to the Marlboroughs? Will you abandon your poor mistress to that harpy? Have you no feelings, lass?"

"My poor mistress is a good deal tougher than people think. It was you yourself, Harley, who first told me that. Royalties are different from the rest of us. She will survive."

"Then all the things I have worked for must go for nothing? And poor old England will be left to the tender mercies of that marauding couple? You'll let Marlborough wade on through oceans of blood to become the military dictator of Europe?"

"But I'm tired, Harley. I'm tired! I can't stand the constant battle. How do I know what's best for England? How do I even know what's best for the Queen? She loved her Mrs. Freeman once. Maybe she can love her again!''

Masham now pushed himself into the argument. "You might consider someone besides yourself, Abigail. How do you think I stand in all this? It was because of you that I put all of my eggs in the Queen's basket. Do you think I could not have married a woman of property? Do you think Prince George would have done nothing for a favorite groom? Why, I could have been a colonel by now, or higher. But, no, I took *you* — without a penny. Your only fortune was the Queen's favor. How can you go back on me now? Why, it's as if you were to take the coins of a dowry and fling them in the Thames before my very eyes!''

"I can't help it! I can't stand in the way of the Captain-General! How can you ask me to, you, his officer?''

"Don't be silly. I'm not his officer. But I see how it is. You were always in love with him, and now you want to ruin me out of spite that you can't have him!''

But the vision of the Duke was too firmly in my mind for me to bother with such trashy talk. My husband and even Harley seemed small, petty, ranting men in contrast. I felt that I did not care what happened to me anymore, if I could only remove myself as an impediment to England's hero. To *my* hero! For he was that again, all of a sudden, and the lines of Cassius throbbed in my mind:

> *Why, man, he does bestride the narrow world*
> *Like a Colossus, and we petty men*
> *Walk under his huge legs and peep about*
> *To find ourselves dishonorable graves.*

Harley rambled on about the rights of Englishmen and the horrors of war, and Masham threatened me with poverty and disgrace, warning me that his father, who despised my low birth and fortune, would never take us in. I do not know what we all might have ended saying to each other had there not suddenly been a loud knock at the door.

It was an usher from the Prince. My husband was sent for. All the Prince's household were sent for. The poor man was gravely ill.

11

*I*t was soon known that George of Denmark was dying. The Queen would hardly leave his bedchamber. The dear, unfortunate man, as patient in agony as he had been complacent in health, lay motionless and speechless, emitting no sound but his stertorous breathing, surrounded by doctors who, I very much fear, only tortured him. The Queen, her eyes misty with sorrow, sat in an armchair by the window, her hands playing with her bandages. In the intervals when the doctors spared their patient, she moved to the bedside so that she could hold the Prince's hand.

When I went in to sit by her side, her first thought was of my condition.

"Are you well enough, my dear, to be up?"

"Oh, yes, ma'am, quite well enough. Pray don't think of me at such a time."

"But of course I do. How is your little daughter?"

"Oh, she has her wet nurse. She is content."

"Would it were so with my poor husband! Oh, Masham, do you know I never had an unkind word from him?"

"Not even the lowest of his servants had."

"That's true, isn't it? He was so good to all. A kind of saint, in his way. People don't know that, Masham. Oh, people close to him do, like you and Mr. Masham, yes. But not people generally. Not my subjects. They thought he was dull and colorless because he wasn't always showing off. You know that terrible remark of my uncle's about trying him drunk and trying him sober?"

"I am surprised that anyone would have repeated *that* to Your Majesty."

"Well, the Duchess, you know, had a theory that royalty should be told everything. And do you know something else, Masham? The Prince *knew* how they felt about him. He knew that King William was being intentionally rude to him when he went to Ireland to serve under him in the Battle of the Boyne. But the Prince always pretended not to notice. Do you know why? Because he wanted to protect *me*! And when I succeeded to the crown, all that he cared about was to keep out of the public attention and to avoid arousing the jealousy of my people. He believed that he could help me, not to rule, but to survive. By just *being* there. By just loving me. And he sustained me, Masham. How shall I live without him?"

Perhaps I should have said something about the Prince's spirit being always present to give her sustenance, but it would have been artificial, and I had never been artificial with the Queen. I was like Sarah in this one respect: I was always truthful. The difference was that I didn't feel I had to say everything: disagreeable truths I could keep to myself. "Mrs. Still" had never been a hypocrite. What the Queen, I believe, valued in me above aught else was my sentient silence. She loved to ramble on, almost as if talking to herself. But it would have given her no solace had she really been talking to herself.

"People think the Prince was indifferent to politics, that he cared for nothing but hunting. But it was not true. He took a great interest in everything that went on. It was only to avoid embarrassing me that he professed political neutrality. But he cared, Masham! Oh, he cared! And he had noble standards, nobler than mine, and certainly far nobler than my sister's. His heart ached over my father. You know the old story, how he kept repeating 'I can't believe it!' to King James, as the word came in of each new desertion from the crown. And how, when he himself at last deserted to join me and Mary, my father retorted: 'What, has old "I can't believe it" gone, too?' Well, that story almost killed the poor Prince. He would have gladly stayed with the King to the end; he would have willingly laid down his life for him; but because he knew *I* had gone with the Marlboroughs to declare for William, he believed that his place was at my side!"

The Queen and I both looked up now as three doctors silently approached her chair. It was not necessary for them to speak. The gravity of their long countenances told their message. My poor mistress, with a loud cry, arose and staggered across the room to throw herself on her husband's body.

✠

Two days later I stood with the Queen's ladies in the corridor outside the chamber where the Prince's body lay, listening to the loud colloquy, loud at least on the Duchess's side, between the Queen and her Mistress of the Robes.

"But Your Majesty must not remain another night in a palace where a royal demise has occurred!"

"Was it not the great Elizabeth, Duchess, who said: 'The word "must" is never used to princes'?"

"But it's the custom, ma'am, to remove from a palace under these circumstances!"

"Do we not make the customs?"

"Hardly, in a case like this. It's not seemly! You should not shock your subjects, who are grieving for you."

"*Are* they grieving for me?"

"Indeed they are. *I* certainly am. But even if Your Majesty does not care what we think, she should consider how the Prince would have felt. Surely no man breathed who had a greater deference for good manners and established usage!"

My heart ached for my poor mistress. Yet there was something awe-inspiring in the relentlessness of the Duchess. Perhaps in her own odd way she had some real feeling for the Queen, but her lack of imagination where other persons were concerned was profound, abysmal, bottomless. There was no humanity in her — except, perhaps, for Marlborough.

Her last point, at any rate, hit the Queen.

"That is true," the feebler voice came to us. "The Prince always did the right thing."

"Then, I beg you, ma'am, to consider what I am asking."

"Very well, then. We shall consider it. But we must rest now." There was a pause, and then her next words formed a cold, clear command. "Send Masham to me, Duchess!"

How I still hear the sweet, silvery tone of those words! I remember how my eyes filled with instant tears and how my knees shook. That was the end of my resolution to leave the court. I knew that I should never leave it now, so long as my mistress lived and needed me. She had lost her husband; she had lost all her babes; she should certainly not lose any love or care or consolation that *I* could offer her. She was alone; I was alone. Even if she was a great monarch and I a nobody, we could share, perhaps even a bit dissolve, our common loneliness.

I looked up proudly now as the Duchess faced me. I met her stare of hatred with defiance.

"I suppose you heard what she said, Masham. You always do!"

I curtsied deeply and followed her to the Queen. I could afford that last reverence to the Mistress of the Robes and Groom of the Stole. I knew that she had lost her war.

PART TWO

12

*T*here now occurred a lull in my life, lasting from the Prince's death to the middle of the year 1710, during which I enjoyed something resembling content. The magnificent Duchess, although retaining her positions as Mistress of the Robes and Groom of the Stole, with all their emoluments, virtually gave up coming to court. The Queen was perfectly willing to allow her to retain her privileges so long as she did not insist on her duties. Sarah's absence was peace at a price! Of course, at court we were never unaware of what she was up to. Whether she was reviling her poor architect at Blenheim, or bludgeoning the Whig leaders, or carrying on her private feuds with other great peeresses, the reverberations were bound to echo down the quiet corridors of Windsor or Kensington. But she was like a storm in another county; we heard the rumble and saw the flashes of lightning; we were never soaked.

I had begun to feel a new confidence in my relationship with the Queen. I was constantly in her company now, and frequently alone with her, and I loved to listen to her memories of bygone monarchs: her charming uncle Charles, with his ugly Portuguese Queen and beautiful mistresses; her somber father, with his beautiful Italian Queen and ugly mistresses; her imperious sister, Mary, and her surly brother-in-law, Dutch William. The Queen never forgot either a kindness or an injury; those of her relatives who had found her dull and phlegmatic would have been astonished to learn how vividly their words and actions, nay, their very tones and gestures, had been recorded in the memory of this silent, watching woman. But where Anne Stuart was not like other royalties — or like other Stuarts — was in her concern for those around her. I existed not only as an audience. She wanted to be told all about *my* life and my small but rapidly expanding family.

I should make it clear that I was not the only person to enjoy the Queen's confidence. She also saw a good deal of the lively and beautiful Duchess of Somerset. The Queen, like many quiet persons, had an occasional need for chatter and noise, and the heiress of the Percys fulfilled some of Sarah's old functions. I know that she discussed politics with the Queen, while I, at least at that time, never did. I could have done so, of course, for Harley and St. John kept me abreast of matters of state, but I fancied — and I believe now correctly — that my chief value in my mistress's eyes was precisely that I offered her a haven from the cares of her great position and that she and I enjoyed a friendship where human values replaced those of the court. I even had a kind of vanity that I was a different sort of "favorite," unique in English history, and perhaps the only person, except for the late Prince, who had loved Her Majesty for herself.

Harley, who penetrated into everyone's secrets, divined mine and joked about it.

"You don't seek, Abbie, like the late Father Joseph in Paris, to be a gray eminence. You are content to be merely gray! You see yourself as eminent in that you seek no eminence, influential in that you scorn influence. Ah, but it takes your keen old kinsman to see that you are the most ambitious of all!"

Harley did not care that I would not speak to the Queen of his matters, so long as I was willing to speak to her of *him*. Access to the royal ear was all that he needed from me; the rest he could take care of himself. And, indeed, my mistress continued to find him the most adroit and sympathetic of her counsellors, and was always willing to give him audience when I whispered to her that he was waiting in the next chamber. He had by now mended all the bridges that had been wrecked by his treacherous secretary, Greg, and it was during this period of the "lull" in my life, that he climbed at last to the top rung of the slippery ladder of power. The Queen had dismissed Earl Godolphin as Lord Treasurer, and it was generally believed that she would soon appoint Harley as First Minister.

Sarah liked to tell the world that Harley and I "controlled" the Queen, and it is true that he exerted considerable influence, but no more, in my opinion, than a minister should. As for myself, my sway was largely confined to giving my opinion to Her Majesty as to whether it would be damper in Greenwich or Hampton Court in June, what potted plants best suited the morning rooms, and which poems or comedies were most amusing to read aloud. But Harley's promotion did make one significant change in my life. It gave him the opportunity to perform frequent small favors for my husband, and when Masham was distracted with his own affairs, my domestic life was much easier.

Masham was not then as greedy and importunate as he later became. I had to do at least as much for him as I did for my brother Jack, whose army career was the one thing I cared about. My husband was understandably anxious to increase his own fortune, and Harley was able to offer him some channels of investment through tradesmen in the city, who always kept agents close to the Lord Treasurer to protect their monopolies. As it turned out, neither Harley nor my husband had any great aptitude for business; they tended to remain invested in these enterprises either too long or not long enough. But at this time they were both hopeful, and when Masham was hopeful he could be quite good company. After the birth of our third child and first son he waxed almost affectionate.

The great change in our lives was that we now became fashionable. Needless to say, this was Masham's idea. He had pushed me into obtaining larger apartments at Kensington Palace to form a permanent abode for our babes and their nurses, although we, of course, still had to travel from seasonal palace to seasonal palace. He proceeded to decorate our new chambers with all the knick-knacks that he bore back from his exhaustive shopping tours.

I was surprised at the good taste that he manifested. Far from proving a bull in a china shop, he seemed eminently at home amid the jade goddesses, Venetian armchairs, painted panels of monkeys, red lacquer cabinets and copper incense bowls that he accumulated. It was curious to me that a man with such a tin ear for poetry and with a mind so full of pornography should have so keen an eye for color blends and *objets d'art*. Yet so it proved. Masham made a little jewel case out of the clutter of his bargains and had a thoroughly good time in doing so. He topped it off with a set of Lely beauties, picked up at an auction of the master's estate, which gave a gay "restoration" note to the whole. I sometimes wondered what the Queen would have thought of it all, but she never visited any parts of her abodes that she did not personally occupy.

Having adorned our rooms, the next thing he had to do was to fill them, and Masham proposed that we give a series of little supper parties.

"You and I may not be a dream of love," he told me frankly, "but that's no reason not to make the best of things. Who knows how long Great Anna will last? Don't look at me that way, Abbie! No one can hear us. Wasn't it Leo X who said: 'God gave us the papacy — let us enjoy it'? Well, I propose that we be leonine. There's nobody in this court who will dare turn down a bid from Mistress Masham. So we may be as choosy as we please! I suggest that invitations to our little gatherings of eight will become the most sought after in England. But we'll have to get you properly dressed first, my gal. I shall have Mademoiselle Rose in for some fittings."

"Rose? How will we pay for it all?"

"We shan't, silly!"

When I talked to my sister Alice about this, I was already attired in a new gown of robin's egg blue, which I confess I found attractive, although it was much too elaborately laced.

"But what's wrong, Abbie? I think Masham's perfectly right. Why shouldn't you be decently dressed?"

"It's not a question of decency, Alice. I've always been decent, I hope, even when I was a laundress. But this dress isn't *me*. You know it isn't!"

"You mean 'me' can't be improved? 'Me' can't be touched up?"

"It's not that. It's what the dress stands for. Masham's whole view of our situation is false. He wants me to be alluring and insinuating and all kinds of things I'm not so that he can push himself forward in court!"

"And that's a crime? Listen, Abigail. It's time I offered you something in return for all you've done for me. Of course, I haven't anything to give but advice, but perhaps advice at this point is just what you need. Masham is not a bad husband

— as husbands go. He's out for himself — they all are. But the hopeful thing about him is that he's pleasant when things are going his way, and that's rarer than you may think. Keep him happy, and he should be easy enough to live with. Don't think there aren't plenty of females who wouldn't be glad to have him!"

"Some of them already have."

"What do you expect? Fidelity? In *this* court? I tell you frankly, dear, I'd rather have Masham than nobody."

"Be careful," I warned her. "He has a brother."

"Oh, but a *younger* brother," Alice said, laughing. "The sister of the favorite should do better than that!"

I decided to take Alice's advice and to meet my husband at least halfway. I began to creep out of my shell. We gave little dinners and supper parties in our handsome suite of rooms, with the best food and wines ordered by Masham, who proved as much of a connoisseur at the table as in bibelots. I gave more time and attention to my clothes and was soon almost stylishly attired. In brief, Mr. and Mrs. Masham became the "thing."

Of course, I was always aware that the deference and kindness that even the greatest people at court showed me was owing to my now conceded position as favorite. But just as a tradesman who has been knighted begins to conceive that his lineage must be more ancient than he has supposed, and the heir to a fortune to imagine in time that it has been garnered by his own exertions, so did I find that I had to battle — and not always successfully — with the idea that the Queen had selected me as a companion, not simply because I was *there*, but because I was possessed of a rare intelligence and an unusual gift for human sympathy. And I found also that it was a subtle flattery to my vanity to be simply "Mrs. Masham" among the great names at court, possessed of no estate or wealth or dignity, yet known to all, deferred to by all, so that

I stood out more in my bareness and simplicity than had I been as splendidly bejeweled and as gloriously titled as Cousin Sarah. Oh, yes, I *was* like that barefooted Capuchin friar, Father Joseph, whom Harley had cited to me, in the glittering court of Louis XIII! No humble heart beat beneath those plain robes!

My high-water mark in my husband's esteem came when I persuaded Harley to take Masham into an exclusive club called The Society, made up of statesmen, nobles and writers with a taste for literary and political discussion. To ensure conversational ease, the members checked their titles, so to speak, in the cloakroom, and addressed each other simply as "Brother." I had had to confess to Harley that my husband's only qualification was his passionate desire to join.

"And quite enough, too, my dear," he had replied with a benign wave of his hand. "He will do very well. Any group of men will welcome a handsome young buck who can laugh at the wit of his betters and offer a tale of bawdry. We're easier than you women, you know."

He was right. Masham, by all reports, was a success in The Society, even with the great Jonathan Swift, who had recently come to court under Harley's auspices. I was learning not to underestimate my husband's capabilities.

Our greatest social triumph was a dinner of twelve that included not only Harley and St. John, but the Sunderlands and the Duchess of Somerset. Unhappily, I recall it chiefly because it was there that I noted the first signs of discord between the first two mentioned. St. John had spoken to me before of Harley's increasing bibulousness, but that night was the beginning of my own apprehensions about it.

The beautiful, red-haired Duchess was at her loveliest and most beguiling. Unlike her absent and arrogant husband, who would not have condescended to sit at so plebeian a table (even for a favorite!), she professed a horror of "titled bores" and a preference for the company of those who perceived the "folly of life" and had the wit not to be heavy about it. She leaned forward now, her elbows informally on the table, her alabaster arms charmingly exposed, and cast those shining green eyes from one to the other of our privileged guests.

"This is what I really adore!" she exclaimed. "Isn't it *fun*? I feel like the 'good' Duke in *As You Like It*. Didn't he prefer a picnic to 'painted pomp'? And what was it he said about the woods? You, my dear hostess, who know everything, can tell us that. What did he say the woods were free from?"

It was like the Duchess to give someone else the chance to shine. I flushed with pleasure as I quoted: " 'More free from peril than the envious court.' "

"Precisely! Oh, good for you! Isn't it so, Mr. Harley? We are all honest at the Mashams'. Honest, that is, so long as honesty may entertain."

Harley, whose usually pasty cheeks were now flushed, raised his glass to me. "It is most true that Mrs. Masham abhors flattery. We must salt our tongues before we enter here."

St. John's jeering laugh greeted this. "Do you remember, Abigail, what Decius Brutus said of Caesar? This Shakespeare game can be a two-edged sword."

"What is the verse, Mr. St. John?" the Duchess demanded. "Tell me the verse."

" 'But when I tell him he hates flatterers,
He says he does; being then most flattered.' "

The Duchess clapped her hands. "Ah, that wins! But, seriously, don't you all agree we're more relaxed here than anywhere else in court? I can't understand people who must always be playing their born roles. My husband, for example: he is always being a duke. Oh, but he is! Don't shake your head politely. *I* should know. He looks in his mirror and sees a duke. And Sarah Marlborough is always being a duchess. And even our revered sovereign spends most of her hours being a queen. Though perhaps it's not fair to cite her. Perhaps in her case one really can't help it. But I couldn't *live* if I had to be a Somerset all day."

"Not everyone, Duchess, has such beauty and wit to fall back upon. Some of us must make do with our labels."

I thought this a bit heavy of Harley, but the Duchess seemed to take it in good part.

"But you, Mr. Harley, would be perfectly happy with your books if you were no one at all!" she continued spiritedly. "No, I cannot conceive the satisfaction that some people get out of mere birth. To cite my poor husband again — don't frown, anybody; he should have come if he wanted to control my tongue — I don't believe a single hour goes by that he does not think: 'I'm a Seymour. I'm a Seymour. My so-many-times-great-aunt married Henry VIII!'" We all laughed. "And do you know that he smiles if you mention a family he doesn't know? He finds it actually comical to exist in a sphere outside the Seymours!"

"I wonder if our Duchess isn't being the superior consort," Harley observed, with a wink down the table. "Can a lady born a Percy be in awe of any other English name?"

"But Henry VIII, my dear Harley — Henry VIII!" The Duchess threw up her hands. "Imagine owing one's entire genealogical distinction to the fact that one's aunt had been sold to that monster! Talk about the sacrifice of the Cretan maidens to the Minotaur!"

"I seem to recall an even prouder boast of the Seymours," the irrepressible Harley continued. "Does not the Duke descend from Catharine Grey, sister of the unfortunate Lady Jane? Surely they were granddaughters of Mary Tudor, your Minotaur's sister?"

"As if my dear spouse would ever let me forget *that*!" the Duchess exclaimed. "He sees not only a duke in that mirror. He sees a king! Oops!" She raised a finger in mock horror to her lips. "Have I been guilty of treason? Will I share the fate of Great-great Aunt Jane?"

"But what is treasonable about being in line to the throne?" Harley demanded. "Parliament has fixed the succession on the House of Hanover, but if that noble house should fail, surely the Duke is next?"

"That is what the Queen told me!" I exclaimed in sudden recollection. "She said that so long as Parliament had excluded so many foreign princes, why not go one step further and bring the succession back to England?"

"An excellent suggestion!" cried Harley. "Why go to Germany for our masters when we have good English dukes at home?" He bowed to the Duchess and again raised his glass to her. "And a duke with so dazzling a consort!"

I think it was the glare in St. John's eyes that made me realize that we were getting out of line. But the Duchess was perfect. She professed to make light of it all.

"Oh, I think we can safely leave the business of being royal to our Teutonic friends. They take it all with such splendid seriousness! The only kingdom I want is one of hearts."

"And that you already have!" Harley assured her.

After our party broke up, and while Masham was below, escorting the Duchess to her chambers, Harley and St. John sat on with me for a last glass of wine. The former decidedly did not need it, but he drank it nonetheless, and St. John made no effort to conceal his impatience.

"You're either going to have to drink less or choose your drinking companions with more care, my friend!"

"Oh, Henry, you're always fussing at me these days."

"Do you call it fussing to warn a man about antagonizing the Elector of Hanover?"

"But you hate him yourself. You told me so!"

"Did I tell the Duchess of Somerset?"

"Surely *she*'d like him out of the way. Did you believe that bit about her not caring for the crown?"

"Not for a minute. But you're dealing with one of the cleverest women in England and a violent Whig, to boot. Every word you uttered tonight will be known to the war party tomorrow and will be used to topple you. Harley is against the Act of Settlement! Harley challenges the power of Parliament to regulate the succession! You prate about wanting to bring peace to Europe, but you'll find there's mighty little you can do in the Tower for the cause of peace!"

"You exaggerate so, Henry. Abbie here will make everything right with the Queen, won't you, Abbie?"

"Abbie's too busy these days being a great hostess," St. John observed sourly.

"Oh, why don't you both go to bed?" I was tired of the argument and nervous about what had been said at table. I sent for Harley's servant, who assisted his wobbly master to the door, but St. John lingered a moment for a last word.

"We *will* need you with the Queen, Abbie," he said gravely. "You can see what's happening to Harley."

"Why does he drink more when he's getting ahead?" I asked fretfully. "One would think it would be just the reverse."

"Because he thinks he sees his goal in sight. Being First Minister! But to him the end of the road is simply ennui. His whole life has been scheming and maneuvering. He's a climber who climbs for the sake of climbing. The peak is a kind of death."

"How extraordinary! But leave me out of it. The Queen doesn't want to talk politics with me."

"We can't afford to leave you out of it, Abbie."

"I'm sorry, Henry. You'll have to find someone else."

"Don't you care about the peace? Don't you care about men getting killed for nothing?"

I looked at him, half in curiosity. I had always assumed that this brilliant disciple of Harley's was out for himself and for himself alone. But no doubt it was possible for a statesman to care for himself as well as for humanity. St. John may have looked forward to a benign Europe with himself as the prince of peace.

"I care about staying in the slot where I belong," I insisted. "I care about doing the job God gave me to do."

"And how can you be sure what that is?" He paused, for Masham had reappeared in the doorway. "Well, do this for me, will you? Listen to Jonathan Swift. You like him, don't you?"

"Everyone likes him. Except the Queen."

"Exactly. He can't talk to her. But he can talk to you."

"He can *talk* to me, certainly."

"That's all I ask."

He turned to go as Masham called out jovially: "If I can help Master Swift, inform me! She's a stubborn baggage, but I know how to move her!"

13

*J*onathan Swift had appeared at court early in 1710, as a
protégé of Harley, and had begun a career for which I can
find no parallel in any history book. He was Irish-born, a
bachelor of middle years, a lazy man, but of prodigious energy
and a one-time secretary of the late Sir William Temple, who
had long represented our government in Holland. Following
Sir William's death he had returned to Dublin and had now
been sent over by the Church of Ireland to petition the crown
for the grant of certain tithes. I do not even know whether or
not he was ultimately successful in his embassy, for this mission seemed to be engulfed in the larger one of his becoming,
for three years, the close advisor and spokesman to the press of
the Tory leaders.

How did he manage it? Even now it is difficult to say. He had
neither money nor birth, nor any great connections, at least

until he had conquered the total admiration of two men as different as Harley and St. John. He was neither soft of speech nor gently persuasive; indeed, he could be harsh and dogmatic, and he was plainly outspoken in an age of the crudest flattery. He was always voicing opinions that were near heresy, in both ecclesiastical and political matters, and although women exercised great influence over our statesmen, he was never credited with — or accused of — a love affair at court. No, so far as I could make it out, Swift conquered the Tories by his intellect alone, by the massive reach of his imagination and by the inexorable logic with which he deduced the conclusions from the phenomena that this imagination encompassed. Men agreed with Swift because they had to agree with him, or seem fools, not only to others but to themselves. Only the Queen held out. She had discovered, unfortunately, that he was the author of *A Tale of a Tub* and could never forgive his sarcasms at the expense of the church.

When, years later, he published his famous *Gulliver's Travels*, which all the world has read, I thought back on him as having come to Windsor somehow as his hero came to Lilliput, except that he towered over us, not by the giant size of his body, but of his brain. He viewed us all with an easy and sometimes amiable familiarity, impressed by nobody and by nothing. I was enormously flattered that, from the very beginning of our acquaintance, made at Harley's evening gatherings, he seemed to find my intelligence large enough to embrace his judgments.

Although his physique was not commanding — he was rather short than tall — Swift's countenance inspired respect. His eyes were sky blue, with a flash of sapphire, and he had a disconcerting way of fixing them on you in a prolonged stare, almost a glare. He had thick dark eyebrows, a large, finely chiseled aquiline nose and a firm, oval chin with a dimple. Although, as I have said, he was not given to gallantry at court (I did not know at the time of his lifelong enigmatic relationship with a certain lady in Dublin), his attentions to a woman were highly flattering, for he seemed just the type of man that would be apt to despise the intellect of our sex.

Swift had made a point of becoming friendly both with Masham and myself. I sometimes observed him and my husband laughing heartily together in a corner or window embrasure, away from the rest of the company, and I suspected that they had a common taste for ribaldry. But Swift, unlike Masham, never showed any disposition to try such stories on me. He was inclined, on the contrary, to be almost too serious. He would come to our apartments of an evening, and if we were playing cards, he would stalk about the chamber until a table had broken up and was ready to talk. He would never pick up a hand himself.

One evening, when he had withdrawn with me to a divan, he quizzed me about my fondness for cards.

"I was watching you tonight, Mrs. Masham. You appeared to be giving the game your total attention. Your body was erect and still. There was no movement whatever except when you pulled a card and placed it on the table with a click. Is the game so difficult?"

"One must remember the cards. After the first three tricks, it should be possible to calculate what each of the other players holds."

"And is this a source of keen pleasure to you?"

"It is a source of pleasure, Mr. Swift. My life has not been so filled with pleasures that I can ignore cards. Besides, whist is like life. You cannot expect to win with a poor hand, but with skill you may reduce defeat to a minimum."

"In chess there is no element of chance. I should think a person of your intellect would prefer it."

"Perhaps I should, were I a man. But as a woman, with so many disadvantages, I prefer the cards. They reflect the struggle as I see it around me: so much for luck, so much for skill. The high trumps may come to the undeserving, but there is always the chance that they may misuse them. And then, too, the contest proceeds so smoothly, so intellectually!" I clasped my hands in sudden recognition of how much I really *did* care for the game. "There is no blood, no squalor. It is a world of form. Or ideals, if you wish."

"No, I don't wish," Swift retorted with a rumbling chuckle. "I don't wish it at all! I see the game you're really playing. May I be so bold as to instruct you what it is?"

"By all means. I welcome candor."

"Then you shall have it! My friend Harley has told me something of your life before you came to court."

"I was a laundress, Mr. Swift."

"But no ordinary one. A laundress with some great connections."

"Those, you might put it, were my trumps."

"Precisely! You were dealt a poor hand, but you had a couple of high cards. And you played them with consummate skill."

"On the contrary, I had great good luck."

"You mean because the Duchess trumped her own ace? Perhaps, but you see it as whist, anyway. That's just my point. Be it luck or skill, you won your rubber."

"The game is hardly over yet."

"When you say that, do you imply that you may still lose? But you may also bid a slam! Aren't you settling for too little?"

"To what do you assume that I might aspire, Mr. Swift? Should I ask the Queen to replace the Duke of Marlborough with Captain Masham and build me a palace the size of Blenheim?"

"It would be an excellent start!" he exclaimed, slapping his knee. "Then we could call a halt to this crazy war!"

"We can dream, I suppose."

"Must it be just a dream, Mrs. Masham? Oh, I know what Harley says about your determination not to mix in politics. But I'm not suggesting that you appoint generals or build palaces. I'm simply suggesting that, as a person of known integrity and respected judgment, you might occasionally let your opinion be known on board this ship of fools!"

Of course, I knew that Swift was cultivating my friendship as a means of access to my mistress, but I found his company irresistible. He even shared the enthusiasm that I had inherited from my father for Mr. Shakespeare, and we had many discussions of the poet's characters.

One day we talked of Shakespeare's kings and queens.

"Do you find them real? You have had more occasion to view royalty from close quarters than a poor playwright ever could have."

"No," I replied, after giving this a moment's thought. "To put kings and queens on the stage as they are, you would have to show the etiquette, the ceremonial. It would be tedious. Shakespeare was quite correct to move his royalties rapidly across the boards. One forgives the error for the action. And then, too, his kings and queens speechify much more than monarchs do in life. Certainly Queen Anne and the late King William tended to silence. Who wants silent actors on stage?"

"But do you find that the personalities of Shakespeare's sovereigns correspond to what you have observed?"

"There's no queen in Shakespeare quite like ours, if that's what you mean, Mr. Swift."

"What of royal counsellors, then?"

I smiled. "There is no counsellor in Shakespeare quite like Mr. Harley, if that's what you mean."

"Or in any play in any language!" he exclaimed with his rumbling laugh. "But are there no characters in our court like the Earl of Kent in *King Lear*, or Paulina in *The Win-*

ter's Tale? Counsellors who have the courage to speak up to their sovereign when he is wrong? Who can cry: 'Be Kent unmannerly when Lear is mad!' "

I reacted cautiously. "Surely, sir, you are not suggesting..."

"That good Queen Anne is mad? No, God bless her, such treason could never fall from my lips. But does she have any around her who would dare speak up if she were? Are there any plain men in court? Or women?"

"Remember what the Duke of Cornwall said about Kent's plainness." I paused, trying to recall the lines. Swift, of course, at once supplied them for me with his customary exuberance:

" 'These kinds of knaves I know, which in their plainness
Harbor more craft and more corrupter ends
Than twenty silly-ducking observants
That stretch their duties nicely.'

"But *distinquo*," he continued. "Cornwall is a tyrant who sees plainness as the mask of a man's resistance to his tyranny. He knows that had Lear listened to Kent, Lear would still be king."

"And you suggest that the Queen may need a Kent?"

"I suggest that every crown needs a Kent."

"Let us pray, then, that Her Majesty may never be in such dire straits as her mythical predecessor," I said firmly, disliking the subject. "Shall we talk of other characters in Mr. Shakespeare? What about Irishmen?"

"There are none. Except in *Henry V*, and that's a libel."

He talked to me, as we became better friends, more and more about the war. I was interested in it, of course, and I sympathized, as what sentient woman would not, with the desirability of an early peace, but I preferred to hear him on literature or history or even on personalities at court, about whom he could be devastating. So he offered at last a kind of conversational exchange. He would descant, fascinatingly, on my adored Congreve, emphasizing the playwright's utter immorality, pointing out that Mirabell, in *The Way of the World*, my favorite of the heroes, marries off his pregnant mistress to an unwitting friend, and then Swift would insist on my attending his argument that we were really fighting in Flanders for Dutch interests and that the war party was the dupe of the ancient policy of William III, who had always placed the Stadtholder ahead of the English monarch. Or if he delighted me with an account of how Wycherly managed to debase a theme of Molière, I had to pay for it by acknowledging the absurdity of the British fear of French domination in Spain, when our own candidate for the throne in Madrid was an Austrian archduke who was striving to unite Iberia with all the Germanies and restore the empire of Charles V!

"Is *that* what you're killing English youths for?" he would demand, hitting his fist against a table. And finally he would direct his attention, hypnotizing me with that stare that seemed to address me sometimes as a woman, sometimes as a senate, sometimes as an unruly mob, to the individuals who were profiting from the war. For there had to be such, he insisted. *Somebody* had to be gaining from it. And it was surely not the foot soldiers who died or were maimed, or the taxpayers who were gouged, or the poor who never cared for anything but sex and gin. Who could it be but those who were paid in the wages of money or glory? Or both? And who had greater such wages than the Marlboroughs?

"You say the Duke has never been beaten, Mrs. Masham. It is true. And if we had a proper war, he'd be worth a kingdom to us. But what are victories in a fight that's already been won? Must we go on until he has laid Europe in waste, and Blenheim is the greatest palace on the globe?"

What could I say? I hated it when people attacked my former patrons. I had suffered too much from the Duchess to be able to join in any criticism of her conduct without appearing vengeful, and my admiration of the Duke was a private part of myself that I wanted to keep away from the world. I had made him, in my Holywell days, into a kind of household god, and he belonged on a mantel in my heart that I had no wish to expose to the sweeping hand of this would-be house cleaner. For would not the vision of those shattered fragments on the floor confirm what was already beginning to be a dim suspicion that my noble idol might be made of clay?

Obviously, I was being groomed for a mission. I began to feel like a schoolchild on a spring day. Out of doors, shimmering through the open windows of my classroom, was the verdant, inviting countryside of my new life. I yearned to be allowed to fling my lesson books into my desk, slam down its top and run out to the fields to play. But only if my teacher would release me of his own accord. I was held, rooted, by that presence.

The reader by now may be curious as to the exact nature of my feelings for Jonathan Swift. Certainly he was never in the least amorously inclined toward me. He used to say that I reminded him of a landlady of his in Ireland, one Mrs. Malolly, and although he was never specific on the nature of Mrs. Malolly's looks, I pictured her as a red-nosed laundress. And I? What did I feel about him? Well, can a woman be in love with a mind? I never had the carnal desires for Swift that I initially had for Masham. Yet I would have followed him across the African desert. I wanted . . . how can I put it? I wanted somehow to be a part of him. I wanted to obliterate Abigail Masham and be all Swift. I was like an Eastern mystic whose idea of Nirvana is to blend with the godhead. Swift made the life around me, even the splendors of Windsor, seem unreal, quaint.

Perhaps I may give the reader some inkling of what I mean if I relate the conversation that enlisted me at last in his great project. We were standing in a window embrasure during one of the Queen's levees at Greenwich, watching the red-sailed barges on the river.

"You have surmised that there's something I want of you, Abigail."

It was the first time he had called me that. It was like him not to ask my leave.

"I have been dreading it, Jonathan."

"One dreads an invitation to live. The semi-death of our fellow men seems vastly preferable. But a few, a very few, pick up the challenge. I dare to hope that you will be one of them."

"And what has given you that hope?"

"An affinity between us. I believe you have felt it."

"Something of the sort, perhaps."

"We are observers, you and I. We stand apart and watch the others play their parts. Somersets and Marlboroughs, even Queen Anne herself, God bless her sullen soul. Look at her now, the poor dear mistress of our destinies!" I followed his eyes to where the Queen was sitting, bored and disconsolate, the end of her folded fan resting against her lips, listening to a Scottish divine who seemed to be offering her a private sermon. "Oh, yes, we see them, you and I! And we see them without envy, too. That is where we differ from the rest. We might be visitors from another planet. But we are in danger of the sin of pride. The pride that takes refuge in a passive superciliousness. It could damn us."

"It seems to me that you are active enough. Your words are everywhere. We hear you. We read you."

"My words reach everywhere but where they are most needed."

"You mean the Queen. Well, she *did* read you, in your tale of the tub, and she won't do so again. That was your fault."

"That is why I can reach her only through you."

I sighed, but I knew it was no use. "What must I do for you, Mr. Swift?"

"I have but a small favor to ask of you, Mrs. Masham. Simply that you put an end to a great war."

He smiled, but the fixed stare in which he embraced me was not amused.

"Is that all? And how must I do it?"

At once now he exploded into his theme. "It will be through the Queen, of course. The Queen is the key to the salvation of Europe. I have studied every official act of her reign. She has used her power rarely, but whenever she has done so, it has been decisive. With the patronage of the Treasury she could have a Tory House of Commons. With the creation of a handful of new peers she could have a Tory House of Lords. Then she need fear no repercussions when she dismisses Marlborough and negotiates a peace directly with King Louis!"

"Assuming that is what she wants to do."

"But she *does* want to. She abominates the war! You know that. What must be overcome is her inertia. Oh, Abigail, I have studied you, as I have studied the Queen. The puzzle is solved if you are only willing. And you will have played a glorious role in history!"

"You mean a kind of inside-out Joan of Arc? With you as St. Michael to bid me tell the armies to throw down their arms? It doesn't sound like such a glorious role. And, anyway, I don't think I care for glorious roles."

"Do you think I'm such a fool as to tempt you with worldly fame? Do you imagine I don't know you better? I only want you to go on with your own private game. Your own little drama, played out in the theater of Abigail Hill, with Abigail Hill as author, actress and audience!"

"And Jonathan Swift as stage manager!"

"Well, I hope I shall have some function. Even if only a small one. I shall prompt you."

I was suddenly exhausted, depleted, by all of this sparring. "I fear I am not up to it, my friend."

"But will you consider it?" The Queen had risen to depart, and we turned now to face her. I prepared to curtsy. "For her sake!" Swift whispered. "Don't you want to help her to greatness?"

I dipped into a deep curtsy as the Queen turned to the door. Her eye had caught mine; it directed me to go to her. "Very well, sir. I shall consider it."

I knew there was no point in my telling him the extent of the sacrifice that he was asking of me. He would simply have contrasted it to the conglomerate suffering in a single day on the bloody plains of Flanders or on a sinking frigate at sea. But I was still bitter. My fidelity was the single diamond in the simple headband of my life, and he was asking me to change it for one of paste.

14

Well, suppose I were to take it on? How should I begin?"

I asked this question one night as I sat with Swift, Harley and St. John in my parlor at Kensington after supper. Masham was playing loo with a group in the next room; the sound of their laughter drifted in to us.

"Oh, when we turn to action, we turn to St. John," Swift replied promptly. "He has it all worked out."

"We start with the Duchess." St. John's long handsome features seemed to coalesce into a point in the sudden intensity of his planning. "Once we have toppled the Duchess, the Duke should be easy game. The moment she is dismissed, she will make such a clamor he will hear it, all the way from Flanders. Her letters, her messengers, her agents, will plague him night and day. And it will not only prove his annoyance; it will be his agony. For the man is hag-ridden! He adores his ranting spouse. Mark my words, he will desert his post and come galloping home to have it out with the Queen!"

"Poor man!" I exclaimed. "Shouldn't we remember his military responsibilities?"

"Shouldn't we remember the men who die daily, sacrificed to his ambition and greed?" Swift demanded sternly.

"But what can I tell the Queen about the Duchess that she doesn't already know?"

St. John rubbed his hands. "Ah, we shall supply you with all of that, Mistress Masham. You shall have all the poisoned arrows you can use."

"They mustn't be lies, you know."

"They shan't be! You shall be the judge of everything you are to use. Is that not so, Swift? Milady Duchess is too great a target to be brought down with fibs. She is big enough — God bless her or damn her — to be fought with truth. Did I say arrows? Say cannonballs. Cannonballs of all the outrages she has perpetrated on England and the English people!"

I think I would have given up there and then had Swift not looked at me with that peculiar combination of approval and mockery that was my soul's undoing.

"It isn't, Abbie, as if we were seeking to reduce the Marlboroughs to any sort of disgrace or penury," Harley now put in, in his milder tone. "Even if the Duke should lose his command, he would still have the fortune he has amassed in the war and Blenheim Palace to enjoy it in."

"And a loving wife to come home to," St. John added sardonically. "At least *he* seems to consider her that. In his boots, I'd fly to the steppes of Russia!"

"And don't forget the glory!" Swift exclaimed. "He will retire as the greatest soldier in our history. Undefeated, as you are always pointing out, Abbie! How do you know we won't be doing him a favor by preserving his record? Isn't Lady Luck bound to turn on him? Doesn't he owe the Furies at least one defeat?"

"Ah, but you're all wrong!" I cried, rising in anger. "If you want to do him in for the sake of peace, say so. But don't try to tell me it's for his own good!"

"Mrs. Masham is right," Swift interposed, holding up a hand. "There is no room here for smallness or spite. Nor is there any need to denigrate a mighty warrior or his spouse. Let us approach our task in the noble spirit of Brutus, by killing boldly, not wrathfully. Let us carve up Marlborough as 'a dish fit for the gods'!"

"Thank you, Mr. Swift," I murmured.

"And now to work," he continued in a brisker tone. "We have word that the Duke, who is as great a master of the wrong moment in politics as he is of the right one in war, is sending the Queen his request that he be named Captain-General for life. It might be helpful if Mrs. Masham were to let Her Majesty know some of the names that our Tories in Parliament have been calling him."

"And what are they?"

"Cromwell, for one," Harley put in.

"King John II!" St. John exclaimed with his shrill laugh. "Do you want Her Majesty to have a fit?"

"But that's just where we need you, Abbie," Harley explained. "You will know how to administer the dose so that it is effective without being fatal."

"There is also the Duchess's muttered threat to publish the Queen's letters to her," Swift pursued. "This should hardly be agreeable news to Her Majesty."

"But if you tell her that," St. John objected, "she might find a way to stop the Duchess. Wouldn't it be better to let the letters come out, and then the Queen would *really* have a fit!"

"But that would be painful for Her Majesty," I reproved him. "My first duty must always be to her, must it not?"

There was a noticeable silence among the three men before Swift gave me an emphatic "Yes!"

"I have another idea," St. John pursued. "My spies tell me there's a young Whig in the Commons, one Eggers, who proposes to make the passage of the Queen's civil list contingent on the discharge of Mrs. Masham."

"You're not serious!" I cried.

"You don't know how badly the Whigs have it in for you, Abigail," St. John insisted. "*You* may think you don't interfere in politics, but try to tell them that! They are convinced that you are sitting by the Queen's chair night and day, pouring pacifist treason into her ear. Well, you may as well be hanged for a sheep, my friend!"

"And this Mr. Eggers — he'll really do this?"

"Unfortunately, no. Some wiser heads in the party are shutting him up. But we have a spy in the Marlborough faction who thinks he can spur Eggers into defying them and making his motion."

"And why in the name of heaven should we want that?"

"Because the motion's bound to be defeated, and the Queen will hear of it and suspect the Duchess of trying to control her household!"

"But that's outrageous!" I cried, jumping to my feet. "It's nothing but a cheap trick!"

"But it's true!" St. John insisted. "The Duchess *wants* Eggers to make the proposal. Only she hasn't the means of getting at him as efficiently as we have. Is it wrong to help your enemy do what she's trying to do?"

Swift, seeing my expression, suggested that I had had enough and that they should leave. He lingered, however, for a few minutes after Harley and St. John had gone, to reassure me.

"I know this is difficult for you, Abigail. I never thought it was going to be easy. But I pride myself on my judgment of people. I am sure that you will go through with anything you undertake."

He kissed my hand and departed, while I said nothing. Who knows what small weight may tip the balance of our scales in favor of a particular solution? My mind was a tumult of conflicting ideas when I looked up to see Masham standing in the other doorway. He had been watching Swift and me and was smiling sardonically. It was obvious that he had been drinking and losing at cards, a combination that always soured his now usually effervescent spirits.

"I see there are compensations in not being wed to a beauty," he exclaimed with a rude laugh. "It spares me the pain of suspecting Mr. Swift of lewd intentions!"

15

I had not realized how different it would sound for me to take the initiative with the Queen until I was actually on the point of doing so. I then found myself immediately paralyzed. But the Queen, who noticed everything in her immediate surroundings, at once observed that my lips had opened and closed.

"You have something to tell me, Masham?"

I took a quick breath. "I have never presumed to speak to Your Majesty of the Duchess of Marlborough. That is, unless Your Majesty broached the subject."

"And you have something to say of her now?"

"Yes, ma'am."

"Something that is consistent with your loyalty to her as a kinswoman?"

Now what in God's name had made the Queen say that? What in my tone could have so quickly betrayed a new impetus in my approach to the problem of Sarah? Surely royalty had to be gifted with keener senses than others.

"Something that is certainly consistent with my loyalty to Your Majesty."

"Proceed."

"The Duchess is telling people that she plans to publish her correspondence with Your Majesty."

This was followed by a long pause. The Queen's breathing may have been the least bit heavier.

"No doubt she wishes to place *me* in an unfavorable light," I continued. "She will no doubt try to establish how greatly she enjoyed Your Majesty's confidence before I came to court."

"But will the correspondence not show that the Duchess was possessed of my confidence for several years *after* you were in my service?"

"Very probably, ma'am."

"Then its sudden loss would not seem inevitably attributable to your influence."

I was baffled. Why was the Queen's tone so antagonistic? Then it occurred to me that she may have been frightened.

"I did not mean to imply, ma'am, that there is anything to apprehend from the publication of the letters. But it does not seem to me an act of friendship on the Duchess's part."

"No, Masham. It does not seem so to me, either."

"Had I been so fortunate as to receive any letters from Your Majesty, I should have cut my hand off before giving them to a printer!"

"Thank you, Masham. I know I can trust *you*." I breathed in relief as the old warmth returned to the Queen's tone. "The only reason you have no letters from me, my dear, is that I have the good fortune to have you always with me."

"Then I hope I may never have to receive an epistle from Your Majesty."

The Queen sat for several minutes now in silent thought. I presumed she was endeavoring to recall the different topics of her long correspondence with the Duchess.

"You don't suppose, Masham . . . ?"

"What, ma'am?"

"You don't suppose . . . ? No, she couldn't. She wouldn't dare!"

"If there's something the Duchess wouldn't dare, ma'am, I'd be interested to hear of it."

"I'm sure she wouldn't dare put the foul construction on my friendship with her that . . . that . . ."

"That she had the effrontery to place on Your Majesty's kindness and condescension toward *my* poor self?" As I found my lines in this new role, I felt something like exhilaration. Swift had been right! I *could* do it. "But it is precisely what she will do! That is why I have nerved myself to bring this horrid matter to Your Majesty's attention."

The Queen's distress was now pitiable. She clenched her fists and raised them slowly up and down. "But surely she would recognize that any such construction must shame her as well? And she has her husband to consider. A husband whom she loves and reveres."

"And a husband who is under her utter domination. A husband who would not venture to reproach her, even in the bottom of his heart, if she were to burn down his beloved palace at Blenheim!"

"That is true, quite true." The Queen nodded, frowning. "But, even leaving the Duke aside, would the Duchess not be too proud to allow other persons — particularly other ladies — let us say other *duchesses* — draw from her letters the construction that *she* draws? For, after all, such an odious relationship would of necessity — would it not — involve two persons?"

"The Duchess would not have to suggest the existence of a

relationship, ma'am. She would merely have to suggest the *offer* of one. She, after all, will select which letters are to be printed, and what parts of which letters."

"Meaning that she can juxtapose the coolest expressions in hers with the warmest in mine?"

"Your Majesty puts it exactly."

The Queen's voice rose to a wail. "Oh, Masham, what can I do? Is there no remedy?"

"Of course there is. I should not have agitated Your Majesty with this news had I not had one."

"But what can it be? I can hardly put her in the Tower!"

"That would indeed be drastic. No, I have a simpler plan. Dismiss the Duchess at once from her posts at court! That will necessitate her accounting for all her acts and transactions as keeper of your purse. It will then be in order for Your Majesty to impound all papers and correspondence that the Duchess has received from Your Majesty in the period of her office."

The Queen stared. "That would be proper?"

"I suggest it would even be routine."

"I see. Yes, I *do* see. Well, well." The Queen drummed with her fingers on the arm of her chair. "But to dismiss her from her posts! What an uproar there will be. And the Duke! What will he do?"

"I suggest that even the Duke will have to recognize that his sovereign has the right to regulate her own household."

"I suppose he will. But even so. Should I not be concerned, in demanding an accounting, that I may be aspersing the honor of his wife?"

"Not at all, ma'am. A fiduciary is expected to account."

"Privately, perhaps. But not with impounding of papers!"

"The Duchess has been entrusted with large funds of the crown. She should welcome a public acquittance."

"Perhaps she should. But seizing her letters!"

"*Your* letters, ma'am."

"Aye, but letters I gave her, Masham! When I loved her. When she was my dearest friend!"

Was it sudden jealousy that made me say what I now said? "Your Majesty should not forget that while the Duchess has been drawing thousands of pounds from the royal purse, she has been dispensing a fortune on the construction of Blenheim."

A severe silence followed; the ends of my mistress's lips drooped. "The Duchess of Marlborough has many faults, Masham. But nobody, to my knowledge, has ever accused her of peculation."

I pause here, for the Queen's very just reproof marked the beginning of a change in our relations. I had not intended to imply anything more than that the Duchess, in her high-handed and imperious way, might have on occasion, without felonious intent, jumbled some royal coins with her own. But that is not the point. The point is that I had for the first time moved from the defensive to the offensive in my battle with Sarah, and that the Queen had now taken this in. Hitherto I had been the docile and consoling chambermaid, elevated in private to the position of adopted "niece," a kind of kitten to whom the mistress may say anything, but from whom not much is expected beyond a purr. Such kittens may be loved, perhaps even more than cats are. But when they grow up, they must expect to be treated as cats.

At that moment I longed to return to my old position in the Queen's affections. I knew that I was giving up a unique relation, one where mistress and kitten loved each other, intensely and uncritically. No one else, I am convinced, had ever held that relation with Anne Stuart. I may even have given her a support sorely needed in her heavy duties. But there was now not only my sense of Swift's expectant eyes on me when we next should meet; there was the question whether it were not already too late to retract. *Could* I go back?

For not only was the Queen's attitude toward me changing; mine toward her was. She was already ceasing to be the kindly, sentimental, homely, confiding "aunt"; she was becoming the shrewd, suspicious, stubborn monarch, who was only too well aware that her precarious rule depended on balancing one faction against another. Oh, yes, she might care for me still, need me still, particularly as she detested new faces in her immediate circle, but her caring and needing would be more like what she had felt for my cousin. Or was even that presumptuous of me? Perhaps it was! Had there not been a line drawn between myself and the great Duchess in the Queen's reproof to me about the need for an accounting? Was it not possibly the origin of the distinction since made so implicitly in the public mind between the favorites of the first and second halves of the reign: the bossy but splendid figure of Sarah, drawn, so to speak, against a tapestried background of cannonfire and charging cavalry, and the drooping little shape of Abigail, slipping into the royal presence to take the chamber pot and lurking to purloin the royal favor? The Queen herself may have dimly subscribed to the theory that an era of pygmies had been substituted for one of giants.

These impressions, misty at the time, began their process of clarification almost immediately after the conversation above described, when the Duchess of Somerset entered the chamber with two of Her Majesty's ladies-in-waiting and formed a seated circle for the royal tea.

The Duchess leaned forward excitedly, as one burdened with a great piece of news. "I was so thrilled to hear that Your Majesty is going to make the Duke of Marlborough Captain-General for life!"

The Queen was at once her inscrutable self. "Where did you hear that, Duchess?"

"I hear it everywhere!" The Duchess clasped her hands, as if in ecstasy. "I think it so marvelously underscores the greatest relationship of our time. The general of glorious victories and the royal mistress who had the wisdom to bestow her confidence upon him. Not only for today, but for any number of tomorrows! What parallel is there for it? Elizabeth and Essex, perhaps?"

We all smiled, including the Queen, who remarked: "I hope the Duke may be spared *that* fate, Duchess."

It was impossible to know when the Duchess was serious. "Oh, dear me, she had his head off, didn't she? My ignorance of history is a scandal. Well, let us say Elizabeth and who? Drake?"

"He was a kind of pirate," I ventured. "A glorious one, but still a pirate."

"I wonder who could be spreading this report about the Captain-General," the Queen inquired.

"Why not the Captain-General's wife?" I suggested.

"Because she of all people should know it's not true, Masham!"

"Her wish, ma'am, may have sired the thought."

"Then it's not so?" the Duchess exclaimed, with exaggerated dismay. "Your Majesty has *not* given the Duke the life tenure?"

"I have not."

"But the matter is still under consideration?"

"Why do you suppose I should tell you that, Duchess?"

"Oh, no reason!" Her Grace exclaimed, seeming to clasp the reproof to her bosom as if it had been a compliment. "I had only thought that if our enemies were to know that the man whom they see as their ultimate doom had been placed in command for his lifetime, they would be less likely to give credit to rumors that we were tired of the war and anxious to conclude a dishonorable peace!"

It was hard to know what the Duchess really wanted. I suspected that she was always mentally two steps ahead of us, that she was now calculating both what she would do if the Marlboroughs prevailed and how she would cover herself if they fell.

"Isn't it also possible, Duchess," I now suggested, "that the Queen may hold a stronger hand if nobody, at home or abroad, knows what she is going to do? Of course, even if she should give the Duke his office for life, she could still take it away. But it might *look* as if she were not going to. And why should any officer of the crown wish even to look as if he possessed Her Majesty's confidence one second after he had ceased to?"

"Ah, there speaks our little Tory dove of peace!" the Duchess exclaimed, as if it were the best of jokes. "We know who has been coaching *her*!"

This was a rude thrust, but fortunately it irritated the Queen.

"I'll thank you ladies to speak no more of politics," she said gruffly. "I have enough of that in my council without its spoiling my tea."

When the ladies had been dismissed and it was time for the Queen's nap, she remarked to me with a side glance: "It may interest you to know, Masham, that the Captain-General seems to have anticipated your plans for his wife."

"Your Majesty has had a letter from Flanders?"

Those drooping eyes looked up for a second. Just for the flash of a second, but, fool that I was, I trembled. "I have had such a letter."

"May I inquire if it contains good news of the army?"

"It is not about the army. It's about the Duchess."

"Oh!"

"I don't know if Mr. Harley may have mentioned it to you, but . . ."

"Oh, ma'am, why should he have done so?"

The Queen stared. I had never interrupted her before. "I don't know if Mr. Harley may have mentioned it to you, but the Duke begs me not to dismiss the Duchess."

"What has made him suppose there is any likelihood of that?"

"He may have heard rumors. Everybody seems to be hearing rumors."

Her suspicions made me reckless. I began to wonder if I had anything to lose. "If I may be so bold, ma'am, it seems to me that the Captain-General should have enough to do managing his army without seeking to dictate to Your Majesty whom she may dismiss or not dismiss in her own household."

"Dictate? He didn't dictate. He pleaded." The Queen gave a slight sniff. "Rather abjectly, I thought."

I seized on this. "But is it fitting that he should write to you on the subject at all?"

"Perhaps not. But much may be forgiven a man when a beloved wife is involved. Particularly a man who risks his life daily in my service!"

All the sympathy that I could get from Swift that evening was a shrug of the shoulders and a muttered comment about the day in which Rome had not been built.

16

When the dismissal of the great Sarah came, it arrived, like so many of Queen Anne's decisions, without any warning. I learned from Swift that the Duchess had been given ten days' notice in which to surrender the gold key of her office, and that the Duke, whose sources of information were apparently better than our own, had already arrived in court to intercede with the Queen. When I asked if the Duchess's correspondence with the Queen had been seized, Swift told me that Sarah had settled that issue by promising not to publish it. And yet the Queen had still insisted on her demission! There was an ineluctable quality about the resentment of Anne of England once it had been aroused. She might forgive a wrong; she would certainly never forget it.

For obvious reasons, it was considered wisest to keep me out of sight while the Duke was with the Queen at Windsor, but there were plenty of tongues to inform me of what went on. I blushed for our great general when I heard that he had actually gone down on his knees to the Queen, and I was almost sorry when I heard that all he had succeeded in doing was to reduce the time in which the key had to be yielded. The Queen had told the obeisant warrior that her ten stipulated days were now three!

Returning to my own apartments after the Queen's handwashing, I was appalled to be greeted by my pale-faced chamberwoman, who stuttered out the message that the Captain-General himself was waiting for me in my parlor. I found the great man standing before the fireplace, contemplating a miniature of himself that I had never parted with.

"I have aged, Mrs. Masham," he said with a bow and a gesture toward his likeness. "You, madam, have been rejuvenated."

"Hardly, sir." Indeed, he had aged, though not much. He stood as straight as ever, and his eyes were as clear and calm and faintly amused as formerly, but there were dark lines under them, and his figure had filled out. "I am greatly honored by this visit."

"You guess its purpose?"

"Alas, does Your Grace not know that nobody can induce the Queen to change her mind, once it is made up?"

"Not even the person who helped her to make it up?"

"No! And anyway, I didn't. I'm sorry, my lord Duke, but there is nothing I can do for you."

"Would you if you could?" He actually smiled at me. "I thought we had been friends, Abigail Hill."

"How can you remind me of that," I cried in anguish, "when it was *you* who besought the Queen to dismiss me?"

"That was not personal," he replied calmly. "That was because I had reason to suspect that you were aiding Harley to undermine me in Her Majesty's favor. That you were working for the peace party."

"Actually, I wasn't. *Then.*"

"You mean you are now?"

"I think this terrible war should be ended, yes!"

"Listen to me, Abigail Hill." He stepped closer to me and fixed me with that terrifying opaque stare. "When I tell you that I am able to march to the palace of Versailles itself and dictate peace to the so-called Sun King, do you believe me? A peace that might last a hundred years?"

It was a fantastic moment. The hero of Europe was actually asking me to allow him to win the war! He went on to tell me how vital to the cause his peace of mind was, and how Sarah's temper brought her at moments to the brink of insanity. He said that he had to know, when he returned to Flanders, that he was leaving her in stable condition and that only then could he place all of his mind and energy on the rapid completion of the conflict. When, at the end of his now passionate appeal, he actually touched me, taking my hand in his, I burst into tears and pulled it away. I could not speak; I was near hysteria. I fell on the divan and covered my face.

"Go, please go, my lord!" I gasped.

"Very well. But remember, Abigail, I am trusting you!"

When I looked up, he was gone. I locked myself in my chamber and refused to see anybody. I was terrified that Swift would ask for me. I simply could not endure another scene.

I could not see the Queen until the next morning. When I brought her the silver bowl and ewer, she looked at me in mild surprise.

"You look exhausted, Masham."

"I haven't slept all night, ma'am."

"What has upset you?"

"Oh, ma'am, I've been so worried about my cousin Sarah! Do you suppose Your Majesty might reconsider her demission?"

"Reconsider it? Are you out of your mind?"

"But if the Duke takes it so to heart?"

"Then that, I fear, must be the Duke's problem."

"But will he be able to command effectively in the field?"

"Well, I should hope so!" The Queen's stare showed annoyance. "And if he cannot, I have other generals."

"But not like the Duke."

"Masham, I forbid you to say anything more on this subject!"

"Oh, ma'am, please!"

"Masham! You forget yourself. What's wrong, girl? Are you breeding again?"

When I met Swift that afternoon, in the great hall of armor, he wagged a finger at me.

"Don't you know the Queen never changes her mind? Harley and I will forgive you this once, Abbie. But only because of the abject failure of your treason. You may regain the good opinion of the angels of peace by your renewed efforts on their behalf."

"What makes you suppose I'm still willing?"

"Our hope is that your sanity will return when the mighty Duke goes back to Flanders."

He was right. It seemed that Swift was always right. Glory departed for the continent, and Abigail went back to the drab job of disparagement. But Glory, before it vanished, had to be briefly debased. I learned the sorry tale of how Duchess Sarah, at the end of the Queen's stipulated period, flung the gold key on the floor, and the victor of Blenheim, Ramillies and Oudenarde had to stoop to retrieve it and carry it to his remorseless sovereign.

Sarah's fury almost reached the heights that her spouse had feared. She stripped her apartments at Windsor, Kensington and Hampton Court, tearing out the marble mantels and even the doorknobs. She bore away trunkloads of papers and files and took down from the corridors paintings and portraits that she claimed had been gifts from the Queen. And when she was gone, with all of her loot, she bombarded the royal offices with letters demanding sums, supposedly long overdue, insisting on the fulfillment of old promises allegedly made by the Queen even before her accession.

"Was ever a friend so used in the history of friendship?" the Queen complained bitterly to me. "All I ever wanted was to do things for my beloved Mrs. Freeman. But she took and took and took! There was no satisfying her with affection or gifts or trust or even admiration. She wanted my very soul, and for what? To fling it away! I must face it, Masham. She never cared for anyone but her husband. Not even for her children. John Churchill must be made of some strange substance not to have been consumed to ashes in that heat!"

"It *is* strange, ma'am," I murmured. "No other man in the world could have put up with her. She has cost him more anguish than the Sun King and all his hordes. Or was it her fire that heated the forge on which his sword was wrought?"

17

*T*he months that followed were marked at court by the incessant maneuvering of the war and peace factions for the favor of the Queen. I had learned my lesson about being too obvious in expressing a point of view, but there were still ample occasions, when my mistress and I were alone together, for me to signify a heartfelt accord with her yearning to end the bloodshed and to echo her doubts as to the wisdom of maintaining even a successful commander in charge of a war that he prosecuted with such relentless zeal. I had resolved all of my own qualms now and docilely allowed myself to be tutored and badgered by the increasingly impatient Swift. He could not seem to endure the delay.

"What do you expect?" I would ask him. "One doesn't end world conflicts overnight."

"Overnight! Over decade! It's easy to see that none of your loved ones is rotting in a Flanders ditch!"

"My brother Jack is going to Canada."

"Aye, but it's not so bloody there. The poor savages whom the French pay have only arrows to meet our bullets."

The great event that pushed the peace party into the lead was the stabbing of Harley by the mad Frenchman Guiscard, who did not comprehend how valuable his intended victim was to the beleaguered Sun King. When I visited my wounded friend in his bed of pain, he murmured to me: "I'm not accusing Swift of arranging this, but he would have been entirely capable of it!"

What he meant was that the attempted assassination had been just what was needed to hoist him into the public eye in a sympathetic light. When he recovered, the Queen, without fear of violent repercussions, was able to nominate him Lord Treasurer and create him Earl of Oxford and Mortimer.

It was not an easy time for me. The task set for me by the new First Minister and his friend Swift became more and more exhausting. Everything they did was now aimed at the dismissal of Marlborough. I had to be always on the alert with the Queen, watching for the opportune moment at which to slip into the conversation one of their carefully selected anecdotes about the Captain-General's political ambition. I could not risk seeming too insistent; I could not afford to be a bore; and I had to be sure that my ammunition, when discharged, would not simply create a gap that the Duchess of Somerset could fill with her own explosive material. Add to all of this that I was pregnant again, the fourth time in three years, that my little boy was constantly ill and that I was suffering from chronic colds and headaches!

And then, just when a truce seemed actually within our grasp, the House of Lords, by a tiny majority, legislated that no peace could be negotiated that did not encompass the removal of the French King's grandson from the throne of Spain. Even if, by a miracle, we could induce Louis XIV to attempt to depose his grandson, Philip V, the latter had now sufficient backing from the Spanish people to resist his awesome ancestor.

Swift was beside himself. I had never seen him so agitated. He seemed almost irrational. He called on me at Kensington, summoning me from the chamber of my sick son, to accuse me of abandoning the cause for selfish reasons. When I burst into tears, he relented only enough to offer me his peculiar form of sympathy.

"I'm sorry about your boy, but to me it's one life against thousands!"

When I say that I did not at once throw him out of my chamber, you will realize the hold that man had on me! He proceeded now to tell me of Harley's plan to persuade the Queen to create twelve new peers for a Tory majority in the Lords.

"You will have to fight the Somersets every step of the way, Abbie!" he warned me. "They will struggle to the death against anything that degrades the peerage."

I did not know the full extent of the threatened degradation until the next morning, when Masham burst into my bedroom while I was reading *The Spectator*. He was grinning broadly.

"Have you seen Harley's list of the new peers?"

"No. Is it out?"

"Don't tell me I'm ahead of you for once! St. John is to be Lord Bolingbroke."

"An earl?"

"No, only a viscount. Our new Lord Oxford is not tempted to swell the Elysian fields of earldom in which he now so happily romps."

"St. John will resent that. How can Harley be so shortsighted?"

"Don't forget he has the Queen to cope with. She can be very stingy with her peerages."

"Who else is named?"

"The rest are all barons."

"That makes sense. Why should Her Majesty create earls and viscounts when barons have an equal vote?"

"That is precisely the way Oxford put it to me."

"You seem very intimate with him these days."

"Oh, we imbibe together!"

"I don't think you should encourage that weakness in him, Mr. Masham. It's bad enough in anyone, but a crime in a minister."

"A crime? Pray speak more gently of your benefactor."

"*My* benefactor! What do I owe Harley? The obligation, it seems to me, is quite the other way round."

"The Earl of Oxford and Mortimer, in his infinite wisdom, has seen fit to include your humble servant's name in the proposed list. Greetings, Baroness Masham of Oates!"

I crumpled *The Spectator* in my agitation and pulled my sheet about me to warm my now shivering shoulders.

"But that's absurd!" I cried. "I can't be a peeress! Her Majesty will never hear of it. A baroness wouldn't be permitted to do the things in her bedchamber that I do."

"Then you must quit them."

"Quit them? But I don't want to quit them! They are the whole basis of my friendship with the Queen!"

"You had better get another basis, then. For Lady Masham is what you're going to be, lass, and that's that. My Lord Treasurer has spoken."

"But the Queen has not spoken."

"And *you* haven't spoken to the Queen. Is that what you mean?"

"You always absurdly exaggerate my influence with her."

"Do I now? And how did your brother Jack get command of that Canadian expedition, I'd like to know? Through his military reputation?"

"Jack deserved that," I cried, stung. "Jack has proved himself a brave and capable officer. And his engagements have been with the enemy, not with sluts in the streets of Windsor!"

"Hoity-toity! But I know your opinion of me. You'd forgo the pleasure of being a peeress to keep me from being a peer. But get this straight, Mrs. Masham. You shall *not* speak to the Queen. That's an order from your husband!"

I closed my eyes and counted to ten. It was no time to lose my composure. "Let me try to explain," I said in a calmer tone. "You know that I have been trying to help Lord Oxford and St. John with the Queen. It has involved my putting myself in opposition to the Marlboroughs. In view of my obligations to the Duchess and my sincere admiration of the Duke, this has been a source of some anguish to me. Surely you can see that I must not profit by their fall? Would you even wish to yourself? Would you want people to say that Sam Masham shot down their hero for a peerage?"

Masham's face became mottled with anger as I spoke. When I had finished, he broke into a loud jeering laugh, a kind of bray. "Well, if that isn't gall! To build up your scheming into a noble sacrifice for world peace! Look, I *know* you, Abigail Hill! I'm married to you. Are you so lunatic as to believe I'd swallow all that? Do you think I can't see that your whole life has been dedicated to the destruction of the Marlboroughs? Because you can never forgive the Duchess for being the great lady who found you in the gutter and was fool enough to pull you out! Or the Duke for not responding to your stale virginal lust!"

Even at such a moment I was able to reflect that the only truly appalling aspect of his charges was that he believed them. It was not what *I* was that made me feel suddenly ill; it was what I had married.

"Very well," I murmured. "There is no use in any further discussion."

"You'll just disobey me and go to the Queen? And request

that I be taken off the list of peers; is that it?" Masham's smile was now sly. "Don't you think you had better first ask what *I* shall do?"

"What will you do, Mr. Masham?"

"I also shall go to the Queen. And I shall tell Her Majesty how Robert Harley and his minions have trained you from the beginning in your bedchamber duties. How you report back your conversations with your supposed mistress to your actual masters. How Mr. Swift instructs you how to rub the royal back and St. John how to swab the royal hands; how . . ."

"And how do you suppose Her Majesty will react to the person who so illuminates her?" I interrupted him.

"Harshly, no doubt. She will have no further use for either Masham."

"So you'll cut off your nose to spite your face?"

"No, my girl, I'll cut off *your* nose!" he replied with a dreadful shriek of laughter. "That shiny red proboscis that butts into everybody's business but its own!"

I was cornered. I doubted that he would really go to the Queen, or even that he would succeed in getting an audience if I opposed it, but how could I take the chance? It was not the ruin of my own favor — I was beginning to think that might be a blessed relief — it was the prospect of the pain that his lies would inflict on my poor mistress. The little sheltered corner that I had tried to build in her stormy life would be smashed to bits.

"And suppose I do as you say?" I asked. "How do I know that you won't want to be a marquis next week? Or even a duke?"

"Because a barony will quite content me. A barony and the few little business ventures that Harley and St. John like quite as much as I do."

At the hand-washing the following morning, the Queen looked at me in mild reproach.

"I suppose this will be the last of your ablutions, Lady Masham."

"Oh, ma'am, may I crave a favor?" I had decided to dramatize my point by falling to my knees. "Promise me that I may retain my old functions! If there were any way I could dissociate myself from my husband's title, I would, but there is no way. Yet surely Your Majesty, as the fountain of honor, may prescribe the court duties of her peers. Let me beg that mine may continue!"

"Your prayer is granted, my dear," my mistress replied, at once placated. "If Masham has any objection to his wife's having such humble tasks, he can discuss the matter with *me*!"

The other women of the bedchamber tittered at this, and I kissed Her Majesty's hand and assured her that Masham was only too proud to have me serve her in the very humblest capacity.

"We are sure of it," the Queen continued in her most complacent tone. "And we look forward to fewer interruptions in your schedule of duties. For your husband's is not the only elevation of the day. Another friend of yours has accepted promotion. Not as a peer, to be sure, but in the church. Mr. Swift will become a dean of cathedral."

I arose, clasping my hands in excitement and dismay. "At St. Paul's, ma'am?"

"Well, no. Not St. Paul's. We could hardly consider a man of his published views in quite so public a post. No, Mr. Swift has accepted the deanship of St. Patrick's."

My heart fell. "And may I ask where St. Patrick's is, ma'am?"

"Where its name suggests. In Dublin. Where Mr. Swift comes from. And where he will be happy to return. I think it most appropriate."

It was thus that the soul-destroying message was delivered! Her Majesty's blandness was disingenuous.

"Will he be leaving soon, ma'am?"

"As soon as my Lord Oxford, who seems strangely dependent on his advice, can spare him."

✣

A few weeks later, the House of Lords, fortified by the dozen new members, including Baron Masham, voted in favor of the negotiation of a peace that would not have to guarantee a non-Bourbon monarch in Madrid. And then, even while we were still rejoicing, the Queen had one of her seizures. For two days it looked as if she might not survive. I hardly left her bedside. One night, when Lord Oxford, as Harley must now be called, was in the royal bedchamber with me, the doctors and nurses posted just out of hearing distance, the following historical interchange took place:

OXFORD: We have every reason to hope for Your Majesty's early recovery. However, it behooves great rulers to be prepared for all contingencies. I therefore urge Your Majesty immediately to dismiss the Duke of Marlborough from his command.

THE QUEEN (faintly): If I should die without dismissing him, Lord Oxford, what do you apprehend he would do?

OXFORD: He would peddle the crown of England to the Elector of Hanover and to your half brother, and sell it to the one that paid him most!

THE QUEEN: That is a grave accusation, Lord Oxford.

OXFORD: None knows it more than I, ma'am.

THE QUEEN: And you, Masham, poor faithful Masham. Do you agree?

ABIGAIL: God forgive me, ma'am!

THE QUEEN (after a faint groan): You have all been too much for me. Very well! Dismiss him, Lord Oxford! But don't come blubbering to me, any of you, if the French come across the Channel and raise King Louis's lilies on the great tower of Windsor!

18

The Queen recovered, but this did not save the Duke of Marlborough, who was dismissed from his military offices on the last day of 1711. Negotiations were immediately opened for peace. As France was hurting badly, and as everyone now accepted Philip V as King of Spain, there seemed no reason that the great war should not come at last to an end. I suppose I should have been happy, but I had an uneasy foreboding. There was something about the setting of the Marlborough sun that seemed to doom us all to live in the dusk of glory.

I had never much valued glory. Indeed, I had done my little best to be rid of it. But I had had no inkling of what it might be like to live in a world without it. Milords Oxford and Bolingbroke, almost at once, began to seem small chattering figures in the absence of the warrior they had tumbled. In fact, we all began to resemble nothing so much as clownish stagehands fumbling about a darkened scene, pulling at props that we could not quite distinguish in our desperate effort to rearrange the visual effect before the next curtain that would arise . . . on what?

The only man who could have got us through was Swift. The Queen had said that he would stay as long as Lord Oxford needed him, but I feared, now that the Treasurer and St. John were frankly at odds, that Swift would be damned in the eyes of at least one of them for being a friend of the other. When he asked me to walk with him in the gardens of Hampton Court on a damp gray morning when no one else was out of doors, I knew that it would be to say farewell.

"But are there no deanships here?" I cried. "Surely London can't be so small."

"None to which the Queen would appoint me."

I nodded ruefully. Nothing would ever shake the Queen's opinion of the author of *A Tale of a Tub*. And then, suddenly, my heart seemed unbearably burdened. I could not tolerate the prospect of the long days at court with a hating husband and a bibulous Harley without that enlightening presence. The palace behind us seemed in that moment to shrink to the size of a doll's house and its inhabitants to so many gorgeously bedizened puppets. Even my poor beloved mistress began to fade and become dull to my mind's eye. And I? A schemer, a pusher, a nothing! Our human dignity had been only the robe in which this man had temporarily clothed us.

I gave in to my melancholy. I shed all pride. I sat down on a marble bench and sobbed unashamedly. Swift remained standing; on his face was that look of calm comprehension that bore so little sympathy.

"You have awakened me," I complained bitterly. "And now you expect me to go calmly back to sleep. As though nothing in the world had happened!"

"Would you rather I had left you sleeping?"

"Much! I had made my peace with myself. I was happy to be a spectator. I was getting through my life, which is as much as can be expected of a poor thing like me. And now nothing will ever be the same!"

"You're married to a peer of the realm. You're the intimate of a great sovereign. You have your children."

"But that great sovereign is not going to live forever! You know as well as I the state of her health. And my poor children, God help them, are Mashams. After the demise of the Queen I shall have no further voice in their upbringing. You have never seen Oates Manor in Buckinghamshire, my friend." Here I dried my eyes and made an effort to pull myself together. "That is the dismal spot where I shall be immured for life. Once the Queen is gone, Masham will have nothing more to gain from me. He will remember only my low birth — never the peerage that my favor brought him. He will go to London when he wishes, but he will never take me with him. My son will be raised to drink and hunt and carouse with his father. My daughters will be wed before they are fairly nubile to farmers so that the heir may have all."

"And how could my staying prevent that, Abigail?"

"It wouldn't. But at least I would have a richer garden of memories. I could live on that."

"I will write to you, my friend."

It was like him to give me only that. No offer of consolation, no assurance of prayers. He would not insult me by denying the accuracy of my predictions; he promised me only what he knew he could fulfill. And he has fulfilled it — faithfully. He still writes to me. It is my greatest, almost my only comfort.

"I have only one piece of advice to leave with you, Abigail. If the Queen's health continues to decline, the Jacobites will make a last-ditch effort to enlist her sympathy in favor of her brother. Always remember this: that James Stuart will never be King of this realm unless he abandons Rome, which he will never do. If he tries to usurp the crown, he will only bring useless bloodshed to this island. Her Majesty has too kind a heart to leave such a legacy to her subjects. It would be a sordid epitaph to a glorious reign."

"If there is still a task to be done, Jonathan, why don't you stay to do it?"

"Because a man has only so much usefulness behind the scenes. I've used every bit of influence I have. It's time to move on."

I rose, in despair, to go back to the palace. For I could only agree with him.

19

---◄◉►---

*E*verything seemed to fall to pieces. Oxford and Bolingbroke, who had had, it now appeared, nothing in common but their joint resolution to be rid of Marlborough, took to snarling at each other, like two jackals over the corpse of a lion. Oxford was in favor of a conventionally negotiated peace, to be arrived at by parleys between the French and Spanish delegates and all of our allies. Bolingbroke, on the other hand, agile and undependable as ever, sought to by-pass the Dutch, the Emperor and Spain, and to negotiate directly but secretly with Versailles. He was more persuasive than Oxford, and it was his policy that won out in the council.

My old friend Harley seemed now to be suffering from a kind of moral collapse. Whether it was a belated remorse over his treatment of the great Duke or discouragement at the growing success of Bolingbroke's policies or simply the degeneration of advancing age, I could not tell, but it was only too apparent that he was becoming careless of his person, lazy in his duties and even more self-indulgent in his consumption of gin and wine. The Queen was increasingly critical of him. She complained to me that he repeated himself over and over and no longer seemed able to answer her questions. Was he senile or drunk, or both, she wanted to know? I defended him as best I could, but when she told me that he had spent one of his audiences pestering her to allow his son, who had married the only child of the Duke of Newcastle, to be heir to the latter's title, I became disgusted myself. Harley may have been my oldest friend, but our country was still at war.

It made matters worse that the Queen's health continued to decline alarmingly. She had to be hoisted into her hunting carriage in a chair specially fashioned to be pulled away when she was seated, and in Windsor she was raised from the first to the second story on a platform hauled by pulleys. I was obliged to be with her constantly now, and I could see only little of my children. It exasperated me that Oxford should add to my worries by conferring with the Queen only after he had finished a tankard of gin, but when I reproved him for this, he told me to mind my own business.

"My own business!" I retorted indignantly. "And who was it, I should like to know, who taught me to make the Queen my business!"

"The Queen is not Robert Harley, Abigail."

Things had reached such a pass between us that I was reluctant to go to his chambers at Windsor one evening when he sent me an urgent summons. But when I received a second with a "Please, Abigail!" added at the bottom, I decided to comply. I found him looking very old without his wig, and a bit shaky. He was not drunk, but there was a tumbler by his side filled with what I assumed to be gin.

"I don't suppose you've asked me here to be your drinking companion."

"Stop moralizing, Abigail, and listen to me. What is your husband up to with St. John?"

"I didn't know they were up to anything. Except the usual speculations."

"No, this is different. I'm convinced this has something to do with the succession. Something they want to persuade the Queen to do."

"Well, why don't you warn her?"

"Because she won't see me alone."

"And whose fault is that?" I exploded. "Who has been treating her audience chamber as if it were a public tavern?"

Harley's face was like a portrait overpainted with another. I thought I could make out the pink flush of indignation under the pale, puffy mask of his now habitual sadness. "There is no use our going into that now. It must wait for another time. You and I owe each other a few debts, my girl. You can pay off one of yours by keeping an eye on your husband."

"What could he and St. John be up to that's so terrible?"

"That's what I want you to find out."

"Why should Masham trust me? He knows I'm for the Queen before anyone. You and St. John used to be so close. Is there nothing left of that old friendship?"

"Bolingbroke has no friends. He trusts nobody. He would have employed a taster for his mother's milk. Oh, Abbie, I fear you have joined them!"

"Joined them? How?"

"Gone over to them. Conspired with them. Profited with them!"

"My poor old friend, you're making no sense." I glanced at the tumbler. "That wretched stuff will be the end of you."

He was moodily silent for a moment. "I meant well," he muttered. "But my means have been foul."

"If that's all you had to say, I shall leave you," I said, turning to the door. "But not to the gin, I hope. Don't forget you're to present the Prince of Savoy to Her Majesty in two hours' time."

The great Eugène, second only to Marlborough among the glorious generals of our alliance, had come to pay his respects to the Queen, and the corridors of the palace were crowded with courtiers anxious for a glimpse of him. The Queen was not feeling well, and she received him in a small parlor with only a dozen present. When Lord Oxford presented the tall, angular, olive-colored, plain gentleman in the absurdly large peruke, the Queen did him the honor of rising to her feet.

"It is not every day, Your Serene Highness," she murmured in her low, sweet voice, "that we have the honor of greeting the greatest general of Europe."

The Prince, who was nearly related to half the royalties of the continent, was not awed by a Stuart. He probably regarded his cousin-german, Mary of Modena, Anne's stepmother, as the only rightful Queen of our isle. This may have been why he now laughed, with a freedom that just missed impertinence, as he replied: "If I am that, it is Your Majesty who has made me so!"

"What does the Prince mean, Lord Oxford?" the Queen asked in a low tone, which I could just catch, turning to her First Minister.

Had Oxford been sober, he might have replied, with his usual suavity: "He means, ma'am, that a compliment from Your Majesty creates the state it confers." But instead he muttered in a thick voice: "I suppose His Highness refers to Your Majesty's dismissal of the Duke of Marlborough. He appears to believe that Your Majesty created a void in glory that a lesser rank had to fill."

The Queen looked much put out and did not address another word either to the Prince or to Oxford during the audience, which was saved only by a flattering speech offered to the Prince by Viscount Bolingbroke. When the company withdrew, the Queen signaled for me to remain. She sat for some moments in silence after we were alone. When she spoke, she did not look at me.

"Your friend Lord Oxford was impudent."

"Then he is no longer my friend, ma'am."

"Did you not think he was impudent?"

"I fear he had a glass too much wine."

"But it is impudence, is it not, to come into my presence the worse for wine?"

"Undoubtedly, ma'am."

"And it's not just today, Masham. He does it constantly now!"

I shook my head sadly. "What can have got into him, ma'am?"

"How should I know? He's always talking about honor. Does he think *I* don't care about England's honor?"

"May I inquire, ma'am, where honor is in question?"

"He maintains that the orders I have sent to the Duke of Ormonde in Flanders are a disgrace to the nation. You look mystified, Masham. Is it possible you haven't heard of the orders?" There was a note of near-hostility in the Queen's tone.

"Your Majesty assumes that I am better informed than is the case."

"Really? I thought you to be more in Lord Oxford's confidence. But anyway, Lord Bolingbroke and I have been disgusted at the endless delays of the peace negotiations. The diplomats talk while our soldiers die. So I finally told Lord Bolingbroke: 'Let us take the bull by the horns. Let us put an end to the fighting.' He agreed, and drew up the orders to be sent to the commander-in-chief. That he is immediately to cease engaging the enemy!"

I clapped my hands. "Oh, ma'am, I knew it! You are the greatest of sovereigns!"

"Well, Lord Oxford doesn't think so. We had a stormy council. He maintained that the orders amounted to a betrayal of our allies. He became so shrill that I had to shake my fan at him three times! In the end, it was decided to send the orders over the Lord Treasurer's protest, and today they have been sent."

"God be praised!" At that moment everything that I had suffered seemed repaid a hundredfold. Did Swift know? Well, he would, soon enough!

"How is one to understand a man like Oxford?" the Queen continued petulantly. "He shouts for peace, and I give him peace! What does it cost *him*? Does he have to stand up and bear the insult of the Prince of Savoy? No, I, his sovereign, must do that. That is what *I* do for England while my Lord Oxford sobs about honor into his jug of wine!"

I decided after I had seen the Queen that friendship required that I pay one more visit to Oxford and see if it was not too late to warn him of the reckless course on which he seemed embarked.

20

*Y*ou are content then, Lady Masham, to see your country become a symbol of perfidy in the eyes of the civilized world!"

Lord Oxford was standing before his fireplace, his lips apart, speaking as clearly and coolly as in his best days in the House of Commons. Two hours had had the effect of completely restoring his sobriety, and I reflected that he was perhaps one of those who become inebriated on very little.

"I do not see that disengagement need be perfidy."

"When our soldiers stand by and see their former allies cut to ribbons?"

"I am a woman, like the Queen, milord. I see things more simply. I see men killing each other long after we have gained everything we sought to gain. The statesmen seem unable to put a stop to it. Very well. Like the Queen, I would simply say 'Halt!' "

Harley's lips closed in a bleak, tight line. "You have been well coached by St. John."

"Why do you attribute to him what I say? Do you assume I have no mind of my own?"

"You *had* a mind of your own, Abbie. But I very much fear you have disposed of it."

"Disposed of it?"

"Sold it!" Harley made his verb hiss, and I wondered for a moment if he were drunk after all. But then I remembered that in a court of vile tongues he might have heard something vile.

"To whom have I sold my mind? And for what price?"

"You have sold your mind to Henry St. John! *And* your soul. In return for a share of the Assiento!"

"And what, pray, is the Assiento?"

"Oh, Abbie, don't pretend to me!"

"I'm sorry, Harley. I don't know what you're talking about!"

Harley looked at first surprised and then curious. "Do you really mean to tell me that you have never heard of the Assiento, or contract?"

"Has it something to do with the peace talks?"

"It has. It's one of our conditions, though not one that we care to talk too much about. The Queen is to receive twenty-two per cent of the South Sea Company's monopoly of the slave trade between Africa and South America."

"Surely she knows nothing about that!"

"You are quite correct there," he said, with some surprise. "Or she knows very little about it. She thinks it a mere formality. Our frustrated viscount, who believes he should have been an earl, has represented to Her Majesty that the clause is essential for the commercial interests, but that she should dispose of her share to avoid scandal. And who do you suppose will be the real recipient of the Queen's share when she disposes of it?"

"Lord Bolingbroke?"

"Right again. But he will not get it all. Greedy as St. John is, even he cannot arrange to get it all. A sizable slice will be peeled off for the benefit of another recently created peer. Not a viscount, to be sure, but . . ."

"A baron?"

"Your husband, my dear. Did you really not know?"

I shook my head sadly. So *that* was why Masham had not been pestering me recently to ask favors of the Queen. He had figured out his own method of maneuvering for royal largesse!

"Oh, Abbie, I am sorry. Is it possible you're as much a victim as I? And I thought you were hand in glove with those rascals!"

"I swear to God I have had no talks with my husband or with Bolingbroke on this subject or on anything concerning the peace. Since Swift went to Ireland and you took to the bottle, my friend, I have been nothing at court but a bed-chamberwoman. And I intend to keep it that way."

"You mean now that you *know*, you won't do anything about it?"

"Well, what can I do?" I cried in exasperation. "Everyone is always expecting me to *do* something."

"Do you know what happens to those poor black wretches when they are torn from their tribes, betrayed by their own people and stuffed into stinking hatches below deck? The fortunate ones die on the voyage and are fed to the sharks, while the others . . ."

"Stop!" I almost shrieked at him, putting my hands to my ears. "I cannot be responsible for all the woes of the world. First you expect me to end a war, and now I must abolish the slave trade!"

Harley, who had been blandly serious until now, allowed himself a first chuckle. "I had simply thought you might not wish to be the beneficiary of such horrors!"

"Very well. I'll tell you what I'll do. Every time Masham and I buy anything, I shall ask him to figure out what part of it has been purchased with profits from the slave trade. And I shall have nothing to do with that part."

"I see it's all a joke to you," Harley said in a sterner tone. "But I wonder if you will be so much amused by what I have next to tell you."

"Are you absolutely determined, milord, to say disagreeable things to me?"

"Listen to me, Abbie!"

"Why should I listen to you? You want me to do this and do that. You want me to be always going to the Queen to obtain things for you. Why don't you go yourself? I'll tell you why you don't! Because you've allowed your influence to decay to nothing. You go to her half-drunk and bore her to tears when you don't drive her into a tantrum. You give up everything for your sloth and your bottle and then turn to me to pick up the pieces of your ministry!"

But Harley's patience seemed limitless now. "You are right once more. My influence is utterly decayed. The Queen will ask for my ivory staff any day now. But you and I know that she herself is not going to last much longer. Getting rid of me may well be her final act. Which is why I am talking to you now. I owe you something, Abigail. I never forget that."

"And is this how you propose to pay me back? By saying disagreeable things?"

"It is," he replied imperturbably. "St. John has decided that he has no future but under the Stuarts."

"You mean he's for the Pretender? Well, so is half the nation."

"I mean he's for treason, you silly woman! And your husband is with him!"

"Not everyone thinks it treason. I doubt that even Her Majesty thinks so."

"Abigail, you've got to be serious!" he exclaimed. "It's one thing to have romantic dreams about the restoration of James

III. But it's quite another to enter into correspondence with the Pretender and plot an uprising to subvert the Act of Settlement! It is my considered opinion, my friend, after more than thirty years in politics, that this nation wants the Elector of Hanover to succeed the Queen. And when that happens, Milords Bolingbroke and Masham are going to pay for their folly with their heads!"

How could both Swift and Harley be wrong? It was there and then that I made myself face the fact that my romantic espousal of the Stuart cause had been the merest sentimentality. George of Hanover and all things German were too flat and odious not to be true. James Stuart and the Highland legends were so many dreams. Why could I not go back to my chamberwoman days of cleaning and back-rubbing? Had I ever really wanted or aspired to a larger role? If my husband wished to act without me, and to make money out of slaves and pretenders, well let him take the risks that went with the trade. Why should I do anything about it? But when I spoke at last to answer Harley, it was as Swift's pupil.

"How can we avoid such a catastrophe?"

"Good girl. That is why I asked you earlier what Masham and St. John were up to. I wanted to know whether they were plotting to bring the Prince over. But now I see that you know nothing about it, let us concentrate on saving your neck. Let me put you in touch with the Elector. He doesn't trust me, and he may not trust you, but he will certainly use you. You will assure him that you will expend your influence with the Queen to keep her from entering into any sort of scheme in favor of her half brother. And you will put your price in black and white. If you want, I'll draft the letter for you myself."

Farewell to my silly dreams of curtsying before a romantic young sovereign! Farewell to my image of his gracious smile as he should hear me murmur: "Sire, as I faithfully served your sister, so may I faithfully serve you!"

"What awaits us all, Harley? What can we expect of the House of Hanover?"

"Our heads on our shoulders, if we are lucky. But that should be enough for me. If I can only retire to my beautiful library, Abbie, that is all I ask. You see before you a disillusioned man. Disillusioned? The word is hardly adequate to describe a defeat as great as any that Marlborough inflicted on King Louis. For it was my dream to reconcile the Whigs and the Tories and bring an honorable peace to England. I talked to both sides — oh, yes, I talked to everybody — I had eyes in Versailles and ears in St. Germain — I had informants all over England and Europe. I fell into the ancient trap of convincing myself that the end could justify the means. And what do I now find? What any platitude-loving fool could have told me: that the opportunist goes down before the greater opportunist, the wily before the wilier. Henry St. John is handsomer and sharper and more unscrupulous than I. How could I dare believe that if I handed him a knife he would not place it squarely between my shoulder blades? Oh, how I deserve it, Abbie! How richly I deserve it!"

"So what do you deduce from it all?" I asked bitterly. "Should we have let it alone? Would we be better off if Marlborough was still butchering soldiers and peasants on his way to Versailles?"

"Perhaps! Perhaps, indeed!"

"Oh, my friend, you're tired. And old before your time. I'm not going to stand here and listen while you toss my life and yours into the rubbish heap. Good day, Lord Oxford!"

My Lord Treasurer was good to his word, and it was not many weeks before the Duke of Shrewsbury, a principal endorser of the Hanoverian succession, promised me, in strictest confidence, that His Royal Highness, the Elector, was personally grateful to be assured of the loyalty of Lady Masham. If the great Sarah could have seen me then, she would no doubt have felt that she was sufficiently avenged!

21

The Queen was very bad now; she hardly left her bed. Her breathing was heavy, her complexion red, and sometimes her mind seemed to wander. The doctors gave her no more than a few weeks. But when I talked to her alone, she seemed rational enough.

"Masham," she murmured one night as I sat with her when she could not sleep, "there is something very much on my mind."

"Would it help Your Majesty to tell me?"

"If you are still as devoted as you said. Is it not time that I should send for my brother?"

My heart seemed to turn over. "But surely, ma'am, the Prince has been outlawed. Would they not cast him in the Tower?"

"I mean secretly, Masham. Bolingbroke said it might just

be managed. If *you* would help, he could be smuggled into the castle. Only a handful of people would have to know. You see, if the Prince were here, actually in Windsor, when I die, it could make all the difference. Thousands, maybe hundreds of thousands, might declare for him. The Elector would not dare to cross the Channel. There would not have to be any bloodshed, Masham!"

"One can never be sure of that, ma'am."

"Should we not take the chance? For my soul's safety, Masham! Think of the hundreds of ministers who refused to swear fealty to King William, although they had sided with him against my father! Because they believed that even if King James could be rightfully deposed, the succession could never be altered. It was divinely constituted! Mary and William and I could be naught but custodians of the crown until it could be returned to the rightful and reformed Prince!"

"But is the Prince reformed, ma'am?"

"No. But he may yet be persuaded."

"Has he not sworn to the contrary?"

"So we are told, but he is still young."

I buried my face in my hands. Certainly, had this appeal come to me before the advent of Swift in my life, I would have hurried to do as I was bid. But now I knew that the Prince would never become an apostate to Rome; everyone knew it but the weakening Queen. My husband's life was only one of thousands that the conflict would cost.

"I am sorry, ma'am. It will be your eternal glory that you have ended a great war. One who loves you more than life would rather die than aid you in starting another."

"And I thought you were a Jacobite!"

"I am a lover of peace, ma'am."

"Somebody's been at you, Masham! Somebody has bought you for the abominable House of Hanover!"

"How can Your Majesty say anything so terrible?"

"Because it's true!"

I sobbed aloud in my sudden agony. "I have lived for you, ma'am!"

"That's what they all say. But they're all out for themselves. I was used by my father. I was used by my sister. I was used by the Duchess. I have been used by every human being that ever professed loyalty or affection for me. Except my dear husband. Well, I am glad I shall be joining him soon. And I hope and pray that my German cousin will use you all as you deserve!"

I fell on my knees and reached desperately for the royal hand, but it was snatched away. "Ma'am, you are killing me!"

"You, who dared to tell me that you lived for me alone! You're the worst of the lot! Go now, and send Mrs. Danvers to me."

"Ma'am, I implore you! Hear me!"

"Go!"

And that was the last time that I talked to the Queen alone. I continued to attend in her bedchamber; indeed, I was there when she died, but there were always others present.

The day after this terrible interview, when I had somewhat collected my shattered spirits, I sent for Monsieur Le Ménager, the French attaché who was known to be the "secret" agent of the Pretender. I handed him a miniature of the Queen that she had given me years before.

"It is impossible for Her Majesty to do anything more for the Prince," I said in a hurried half-whisper. "The Act of Settlement must stand. But she sends this to her brother with her blessing."

"But Lady Masham, may I ask what cause . . ."

"No, monsieur, you may not!"

"But what shall I tell the Prince?"

"That this interview is terminated."

All he could do was look black, bow and take his leave.

That afternoon the Queen rallied and dismissed Lord Oxford as Treasurer. But to the surprise and consternation of many, she did not appoint Lord Bolingbroke to his place. She named the Duke of Shrewsbury, and the Hanoverian succession was assured.

22

*I*t has been often said that I behaved discreditably, even dishonestly, at the Queen's deathbed. People will have it that I neglected my dying mistress and busied myself seizing and packing up as many valuables as I could lay my grasping hands on. Nothing could be further from the truth. I stayed with the Queen as long as there was breath in her body, and afterward I proceeded, quietly and deliberately, to pack only my own things. It is true that I did not waste my time weeping or pulling a long face. I knew that my future would contain plenty of dark days in which to mourn my unkind but misguided mistress. I owed it now to my unendowed children to gather together all the objects of value that she had given me and get them out of the castle before some Hanoverian chamberlain should turn up to challenge my title. I had not learned about court life for nothing.

King George I succeeded to the throne as promptly and decisively as Swift and Harley had predicted, and Bolingbroke, hopelessly compromised by his treasonable correspondence, fled the kingdom to join the Pretender in France. My husband, pale and shaking with fright, was preparing to follow him, when I astounded and relieved him at once by showing him a letter from the Duke of Shrewsbury, instructing Lord and Lady Masham that if they would proceed to their manor in Buckinghamshire and remain there, a benevolent eye might be cast on any actions in the previous reign that could put in question their loyalty to the House of Hanover. We were also advised that any interest we might have in trade contracts arising out of the late treaty negotiations had been vested in the crown.

Masham's second reaction was characteristic. He threw off his panic as rapidly as he donned his resentment.

"So you have me tied up again, Abbie! Trussed like a chicken on the spit! You cheated me out of a dower, and now you've stripped me of my just share of the slave trade. What devilish kick does it give you to be always castrating your husband?"

"Is that the thanks I get for saving your head from the block on Tower Hill?"

"You saved it only to pitch rotten eggs at it. I'll be in a pillory for the rest of my days. We should have a fine life in the country together, my girl! Every time I spit at you, you'll run to His German Majesty!"

"A woman has to have some protection."

If our subsequent life has been as dreary as I foresaw, it has not been nearly as tense. Rather than spitting at me, Masham has paid me only the scantest attention. We did not even have to fight over the marriages of our daughters, for we had the tragic misfortune to lose them both young. And as my surviving son, who favors his father in looks and temper, has always been much closer to Masham than to me, there has been no occasion for disputes over his education or career. Oh, yes, we have been peaceful enough at Oates Manor. Our exile has never been rescinded.

Lord Oxford did more for me than he succeeded in doing for himself. He was never able to convince King George that he had advocated obedience to the Act of Settlement, and the poor man spent two years in the Tower. He was allowed, however, to have his books there with him, and on the single occasion that I was permitted to visit him (over the vehement objections of my husband, who feared that we would be compromised), I found my old friend as serene and benign as when I had first known him. I think he was actually glad to be released from the life of politics to the life of contemplation, and certainly it became him more.

For a long time I was troubled by the tendency of journalists and historians to classify the last years of Queen Anne's reign as a period of decadence in contrast to the glorious era of the Marlborough dominance. The red nose of Abigail Hill is always set against the radiant beauty of Duchess Sarah. But with time I have become resigned to this. I have tried to recognize that the people have not been given much in the way of pleasure, and that it may be a necessary solace to those buffeted by poverty and plague, by wars and threatened invasions, groaning under the sway of windy politicians and bigots, to have the example of John Churchill's great courage and brilliant victories to dazzle their clouded eyes. He and his beautiful, haughty Duchess were like two stars in a murky sky. They supplied us with an ideal of gallantry and love that helped cloak the carnage and filth of war.

When I went up to London for my audience with Queen Caroline, I attended the public exhibition of the great battle tapestries that old Sarah had commissioned for Blenheim Palace. They were of surpassing beauty. On rich green and yellow fields and hills under cerulean skies officers peered through glasses, troops bravely marched, cannons puffed little balls of white. The figure of the great Duke on a charger, in a plumed hat, dominated one scene. Everything depicted seemed bathed in a rich, golden haze. Everything was ordered and still in the gentle light. It struck me that this was indeed how Marlborough had seen the war. And it was his genius that had made his public view it in the same light.

Unhappily for us all, the military game has become too savage to be left to even the bravest warriors. When the Sun King made his fateful decision to accept the testament of Carlos II and place his grandson on the throne of Spain, he started a conflagration that spread over Flanders, the German states, the Italian and Iberian peninsulas, the Channel, the Mediterranean, the Atlantic and the New World. He was unable to stop what he had started. It was all very well for him to prate of *gloire* and for the poets and painters of France to laud the deeds of his heroes, but what was to happen when they found a bulldog like Marlborough, who did not know how or when to let go? Glory disdained compromise; glory had to fight to the death.

This was what Robert Harley dimly, and what Jonathan Swift clearly, perceived. It took all of the latter's genius to comprehend that Europe could be saved only by something that had never happened before in recorded history: the withdrawal by the victor from the battle. He not only envisioned this; he saw the one way to accomplish it: by use of the royal prerogative — even if the prerogative should be exhausted forever by the act. Anne had the power and the inclination to use it — if her inertia could be dispelled. And for this he had a simple tool.

If I was able to serve his great cause, I should not now repine that my silly reputation has been tarnished, or even regret what will surely be the fate of these memoirs if you, my dear husband, should survive me to read them. As Swift taught me: few people live even once in the course of their lifetimes. Thanks to him, I may have — once.

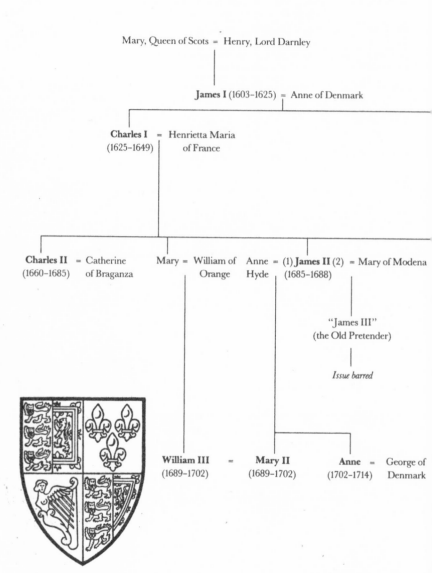

Mary, Queen of Scots = Henry, Lord Darnley

James I (1603–1625) = Anne of Denmark

Charles I = Henrietta Maria
(1625–1649)   of France

Charles II = Catherine   Mary = William of   Anne = (1) **James II** (2) = Mary of Modena
(1660–1685)   of Braganza   Orange   Hyde   (1685–1688)

"James III"
(the Old Pretender)

Issue barred

William III   =   **Mary II**   **Anne**   =   George of
(1689–1702)   (1689–1702)   (1702–1714)   Denmark